A Killing in the Cotswolds
An Emily Swift Travel Mystery

by

Lorrie Holmgren

For information, email Cozy Cat Press, cozycatpress@aol.com or visit our website at: www.cozycatpress.com

COZY CAT
PRESS

ISBN: 978-1-952579-01-1
Printed in the United States of America

10 9 8 7 6 5 4 3 2 1

Thank you to the Split Rock writers' group for their valuable advice: Abigail Davis, Linda Donaldson, Peg Wangensteen and Christopher Valen. I am also grateful to my daughter, Katy Miketic, writer, and editor, for her excellent suggestions.

Thank you to Sue and Simon, proprietors of the Adelphi House in Stratford upon Avon for allowing me to use their names.

Chapter 1

Emily leaned back in the leather sofa and sighed happily as a waiter set a cup of coffee and pitcher of cream before her.

"Can I get you anything else, madam?"

She shook her head. "This is perfect." Across from her, settled in a matching leather sofa, Jack was so absorbed in the newspaper that he barely nodded as a reviving cup of coffee appeared before him.

"He's just like Jeeves," Emily said as the fellow shimmered away.

Jack looked up from his paper and reached for his cup. "He certainly anticipated our need for coffee."

In this gorgeous sitting room with its ornately carved ceiling, marble fireplace and Venetian glass chandeliers, Emily felt as if she were staying in a royal palace instead of a London hotel. A full-length portrait of a beautiful woman in a long white gown dominated the room.

"Ah to be in England, now that spring is here," Emily quoted.

"April," Jack said. "Now that April is here." I'm sure the poet Browning had his reasons for specifying the month." He took a sip of coffee.

"Really? I'm surprised at your poetic knowledge."

"I'm full of surprises. It will take a lifetime for you to discover them all." Jack grinned at her.

Emily was glad she could look forward to a lifetime with this incredibly handsome, charming, smart, and altogether wonderful guy. She had met him on

Madeline Island where they had been drawn into a dangerous murder investigation. At first, Emily was intrigued by what she imagined was Jack's foot-loose and easy lifestyle, defying conventional career expectations. In her more rebellious moments, she had looked forward to shocking her mother with her new boyfriend. Then, to her surprise, Jack turned out to be a physician, who summered on the island and was her mother's idea of a perfect son-in-law. So much for rebellion! Emily did not allow this ironic twist to influence her one way or another. She and Jack became engaged a year ago in Hawaii —a romantic interlude on a trip otherwise fraught with peril.

Jack turned back to his newspaper. Emily poured cream in her coffee and took a sip. It was too early to eat breakfast. She was easing into her first full day in London, delighted to be on assignment for the *Twin Cities Daily News*, writing a travel article about spring in England.

Spring would be a welcome change from the winter Emily had left behind.

Back home in Minneapolis, the snow had been six inches deep and it kept pelting down while Emily and Jack had waited in the airport and another seven inches was added to the accumulation on the ground. Their plane had to be de-iced before it could take off. Emily watched a huge machine blow away the foot of snow that had settled on the plane's wings, sending white clouds billowing into the night sky. March in Minnesota was bleak mid-wintertime.

Yesterday afternoon, when they arrived in London, Emily was delighted to find that March looked more like spring as pictured in calendars and children's books. The grass was lush and green, daffodils were in bloom and birds were singing as their taxi skirted Hyde

Park and dropped Emily and Jack off at the Grand Royale Hotel. When they stepped into the lobby, they had been awed by its magnificence. They took their bags to their room expecting to find palatial grandeur. To their surprise the room was rather small.

"We'd better upgrade." Jack said as he flopped onto the king-size bed that filled the room.

"Maybe later." Emily settled down beside him and put her head on his shoulder. "I couldn't sleep a wink on the plane and now I'm exhausted, but it's far too early to sleep." She snuggled against him. "This bed is amazingly comfy. How can we stay awake long enough to overcome jet lag?"

"I have an idea." Jack pulled her closer.

Now Emily smiled as she recalled how successfully they had combatted jet lag. She took another reviving sip of coffee. "It's almost time for breakfast," she said. "But first I'm going to see what this day looks like."

"You're an ambitious woman."

Emily walked into the lobby and peered out the front door. The sky was gray, and rain fell in sheets. No matter. It would be a perfect day to visit the British Museum. The Rosetta stone, the Lewis Chessmen, the Elgin Marbles all beckoned. Emily planned to offer her readers many delightful indoor and outdoor options for a visit to London.

As she walked back to the sitting room, her phone pinged.

"Emily, I need your help."

Although the caller didn't identify herself or engage in pleasantries, Emily recognized her friend Vivian's voice and remembered that she must call her by her new name, "Vanessa."

"Something dreadful is about to happen."

"Uh oh." Emily saw her plans for a quiet afternoon at the British Museum poring over the Lewis Chessman fading away. She sank down on the sofa. "What's wrong?" Emily asked. Vanessa sounded uncharacteristically anxious. Her friend had always been in complete command of any situation.

"I'll tell you over tea at Fortnum and Mason. My treat."

"How kind." Vanessa's offer shed a whole new light on the matter. Visions of cucumber sandwiches, scones and clotted cream replaced those of the Chessmen. "This must be serious. What happened?"

There was a long pause, a deep sigh, then Vanessa said, "A very dear friend of mine may be arrested for murder at any minute. I'm afraid she's really landed herself in the soup this time. I need your expertise."

"I'll try to help. But I can't imagine how. Surely it's a job for the police."

"Just wait until you hear. Meet me at three this afternoon. Oh, and you might just peruse the *London Times*."

Emily couldn't wait to get her hands on the newspaper. She went over to sit on the sofa beside Jack and peered over his shoulder. His manly aftershave recalled clean rugged forests.

"Why are you hovering?"

"Vanessa recommended that I check out the headlines relating to murder."

"Hmmm. What a strange request."

"Just let me take a peek at the front page." Emily deftly plucked the front page from under the section Jack was reading. "Here it is. 'Murder by Snakebite Suspected in MP's Death.' That must be it. Vanessa expects one of her friends will be charged."

"Vanessa's your posh friend whose manor house we plan to visit, right?

"Yes, my childhood friend Vivian, who has renamed herself Vanessa, is now married to a British lord."

"Why would she be chums with a snake-charmer killer? Surely such a person would be found in a sideshow or carnival, not among the British aristocracy."

"The victim was an MP, a Member of Parliament. So, it's a posh murder after all. Let me read further."

"Edward Westley, M.P., was found dead in his bed in a Cotswold inn yesterday morning. Several snakes were discovered slithering about his body and are presumed by this reporter to have delivered the fatal strike. The police, however, refuse to speculate until the coroner has examined the body."

"I would stay well away from a killer who has attack-snakes at his disposal," Jack advised.

"Of course. I hate snakes. I can't imagine why Vanessa thinks I can help her, but she wants me to join her for tea at Fortnum and Mason and perhaps a bit of shopping."

"I hope you're not planning to get involved in this particularly gruesome murder." Jack shook his head. "But, of course, you are, my darling. What was I thinking?"

That afternoon when Emily stepped off the elevator at Fortnum and Mason, the famous London department store, she heard piano music, appropriately enough, "Tea for Two." She smiled at the tuxedo-clad pianist as she walked past him into the Diamond Jubilee Tea Salon where she found Vanessa waiting for her at a table laden with treats.

"My dear, I'm so glad you could come. I've been in such a dither. As you can see, I took the liberty of ordering our tea."

"Marvelous," Emily said, hugging her old school chum.

"I hope you approve of my choice." Vanessa was tall, broad shouldered, with strong features. Her brown hair was swept back from her face, revealing large pearl earrings. She wore a tweed jacket over a pale-yellow sweater.

"I do heartedly approve." Ravenous as she was, Emily was delighted by the teatime treats Vanessa had chosen. On one three-tiered tray were scones, lemon curd, strawberry preserves, and clotted cream. On another, were four kinds of finger sandwiches—curried egg, salmon, cucumber and coronation chicken. The top tier was filled with little confections of chocolate, passion fruit, mango and violet.

"This room has special memories for me. I was here when Her Majesty Queen Elizabeth formally opened the salon. The Duchess of Cornwall—Camilla, you know—and the beautiful Duchess of Cambridge were there. Everyone adores Kate."

Vanessa spoke as if they were her intimate friends, which Emily was pretty sure was not the case.

A server came with a pot of Jubilee Afternoon Tea. He held a strainer over Emily's cup and poured, then left the beautiful china teapot on the table.

"This is very elegant," Viv...Oops. Sorry, Vanessa! Sometimes I slip back in time."

"No worries, Emily. You do quite well, especially considering you knew me as Vivian for years. I always hated that name. What was my mother thinking? Can you imagine looking at a sweet little baby and saying, 'Yup, she looks just like a Vivian?' And the nuns never let us use nicknames, so I was stuck with it at school.

"Once I complained to Sister Mary Margaret and she told me I should be proud to be named after a virgin martyr. St. Vivian resisted attempts to seduce her, so she was killed, and her body was put out to be torn apart by wild beasts, but they wouldn't touch her. My reaction was 'Ewww.' Sister was not amused. She poked me in the back with her bony finger. Thank goodness those days are long behind us." Vanessa reached across the table and patted Emily's arm. "I'm so glad you're here, Emily. I miss you."

"It's wonderful to see you too. It's been way too long."

"How exciting that you're engaged. Let me see your ring." Emily held out her hand. "Lovely," Vanessa said, admiring the sapphire set between two diamond chips. "I can't wait to meet Jack. Tell me all about him; how you met, what he's like."

Emily gladly sang his praises until she was out of breath.

"Have you set the date? I want to make sure it's on our calendar."

"Not yet." Emily took a scone and slathered it with lemon curd and clotted cream. "You were so kind to invite me here. This is a delicious tea."

"Believe me, my motives are entirely selfish. But, my dear, you must promise not to tell a soul what I have to say."

Emily found it hard to give her promise with her mouth so full of scone. Finally, after rapid chewing and swallowing, she was able to assure Vanessa. "My lips are sealed."

"Good. I owe a good deal to my friend Sophie. She is the guiding force behind Vindi Cat, a marvelous service for helping people who have suffered great wrongs. Now, however, I'm afraid she will be suspected of inflicting harm herself. It is horribly ironic. I'm sure she's completely innocent."

"How do you know?" Emily selected a cucumber sandwich. It hadn't taken her long to wolf down the delicious scone.

"First, you must understand the nature of her business. If I just blurt it out, I'm afraid you'd be prejudiced against her. I'd really like you to meet Sophie."

"I'm here on business as well as pleasure. Did I tell you? I'm writing an article about springtime in England." Emily didn't want Vanessa to think she would be free to devote all her time to whatever hare-brained scheme she had in mind.

"You did tell me and that's why I thought this would work out perfectly. Sophie's office is right here in London. I know a perfectly marvelous pub nearby that your readers would love. You can meet Sophie, hear her story first-hand and incorporate this unusual pub into your article."

Emily's curiosity was piqued. "Well, maybe, but I don't see how—"

Vanessa interrupted her. "So far Sophie hasn't been arrested. But you'd better meet her soon. I do think she might be."

"Why is she under suspicion?"

"The victim's wife was one of her clients. I believe the police will think Sophie was overzealous."

"How curious! Surely your friend wouldn't put poisonous snakes in a man's bed on his wife's behalf."

Vanessa did not cry, "Of course, not!" as Emily expected. Instead she took a passion-fruit confection. "These are so delicious. You simply cannot have a more fabulous tea anywhere in England."

Emily thought this assertion would require more research before she embraced it. She envisioned many teatimes before she could decide.

"Sophie has helped many women achieve peace," Vanessa said.

"You among them, I suppose?"

"Oh yes." Vanessa lowered her eyes.

Emily waited. She looked around the elegant room with its white walls and tablecloths, turquoise china, and fresh flowers. The tinkling laughter of well-dressed women rose over the music of the piano.

She allowed the silence to lengthen but to no avail.

Vanessa was clearly not ready to share her no-doubt sensational tale, but she tiptoed about the edge of it. "Vindi Cat is quite hush, hush. That's Sophie's …. enterprise… I suppose you could call it."

"Tell me more. I won't repeat a word."

"Not now," Vanessa said. "I'll let you know where and when Sophie can meet you tomorrow. She'll explain."

Back at the Grand Royale Hotel, Emily joined Jack who was settled on the leather sofa reading *The Tatler*. He looked like a British gentleman ensconced in his favorite club.

"You look remarkably pleased," Jack said. "Did Fortnum and Mason live up to its reputation?"

"Yes indeed," Emily held out a turquoise box that contained the Brandenburg cake she had chosen as her parting gift from Fortnum and Mason. "Look what I brought you."

Jack's eyes brightened as he peered into the box and saw the yellow and pink checkerboard slice of marzipan cake.

"The treats were incredible, but I did not learn all I hoped from Vanessa. Since she has moved to Britain, she's become quite reserved. When we were at St. Agnes Elementary School, she was much more chatty and forthcoming. We often got in trouble for 'visiting with our neighbor,' as the nuns called it."

"Yet Vanessa is the one who called you and asked for help."

"True, and now she wants me to meet her friend Sophie who, she fears, may be accused of murder."

"The one with the snakes."

"Oddly enough, Vanessa did not deny that her friend planted them. I think it's time to do a little research."

Emily went over to the computer conveniently provided in the drawing room for hotel guests, sat down and keyed in "Vindi Cat."

The website featured a slinky outline of a feline, its back arched, fur on end. The text was enigmatic. "We offer closure. If you have been harmed, we offer relief from your anger." That was it. No bragging about past successes. There was a form one could fill out to request a service but no phone number or email for anyone at Vindi Cat.

"Curiouser and curiouser," Emily said.

"Did your friend Vanessa avail herself of these mysterious services?"

"I believe she did, but so far she hasn't explained how. She seemed strangely reluctant, as if she thought I might disapprove."

"If it involved snakes, I'm not surprised. Tell me: how did your friend Vanessa, who once went to school with you in Minneapolis, end up living in England?"

"It's a very romantic tale. Vivian changed her name to Vanessa right after college and traveled to England on a cheap flight. She was backpacking through the English countryside when she strolled into the grounds of a private estate that looked like Downton Abby. Naturally, she was fascinated and began to wander about. Eventually, she became hopelessly lost in the maze, panicked, began running, tripped and turned her ankle. Who should come to rescue her but the owner of the estate, Lord Chillingworth! It was like a scene from Jane Austen's *Sense and Sensibility*. He scooped her up in his manly arms and carried her into his stately home. Of course, he insisted she stay until she had recovered. Vanessa started out trespassing and ended up lady of the manor. When Mindy and I found out, we were consumed with envy. Our old schoolmate, Vivian, transformed into Lady Vanessa."

"Ahem." Jack said with a stern look. "You surely don't wish to be married to Lord Chillingworth."

"Not now, of course. Not after I met you. So much nicer to be engaged to you than to a fabulously rich peer of the realm."

"Hmmm. And I assume Vanessa, née Vivian, has lived happily ever after."

"Oh, yes. Now she has become quite British with only occasional traces of her Minnesota background."

"So, there'll be no hot dishes when we dine at the castle? No lime-Jell-O cottage-cheese surprises?"

"No, her hot dish days are far behind her."

"Now it's spotted dick and toad in the hole, I suppose."

"Golly, I hope not. Roast beef and Yorkshire pudding would be much nicer. We are invited to the manor for dinner on Wednesday. Tomorrow I will meet her friend. Vanessa has promised me it will be at an interesting pub I can feature in my article."

Chapter 2

Promptly at 10 a.m. the next day, Vanessa met Emily in the lobby of her hotel. "Let's walk to the Churchill Arms," she suggested, striding briskly down the front steps of the Grand Royale. "The exercise will do us good."

Emily agreed. She hoped to glean more details about Vanessa's mysterious friend before they met.

The two women crossed the street and walked along Hyde Park's wrought iron fence where the grass was a lush green and fields of daffodils were in bloom. Emily peeked in at Kensington Palace just inside the gate. It was an impressive red brick building where the royals had lived since the seventeenth century. Yesterday afternoon, she and Jack had walked there, going past the statue of Queen Victoria, who stared down at visitors with regal eyes, and through the garden where tiny spring flowers bloomed. In the tearoom they each had a scone with jam and clotted cream and Emily browsed among the souvenirs, tea pots and cups, jewelry, teas and candies and cookies. She looked forward to coming back and going through the public rooms of the palace. She especially wanted to see the famous King's Staircase described by Lucy Worsley in her book, *Courtiers, the Secret History of Kensington Palace*, where painted panels showed 18th century courtiers, gossiping and flirting and scheming.

"It's a thrill to be in England," Emily said. "*This royal throne of kings, this sceptered isle, this earth of majesty, this seat of Mars, this other Eden, demi-paradise,*" she quoted joyfully.

"You still remember," Vanessa said. "Well done, you."

"Shakespeare's words come to mind wherever I go in England."

"Once an English major, always an English major," Vanessa said. "Let's keep moving along. The pub may be crowded. Since it's lunch time, we won't have any trouble getting in, but later on, it's a different story. Absolutely packed. Your readers will love it. So unusual."

Vanessa had not revealed their destination before she came by the hotel to escort Emily to meet Sophie. "I want the pub to be a complete surprise," she had told Emily.

More likely Vanessa wanted to make sure Emily didn't dart off on her own and skip the meeting. In a few blocks, Vanessa guided Emily away from Hyde Park, turning down a street lined with antique shops and patisseries.

"What delightful window shopping," Emily said, pressing her nose against a bakery window, which displayed confections that looked more Parisian than British.

Vanessa kept up a brisk pace. "Step it up, Emily. We mustn't keep Sophie waiting."

Emily scrambled to catch up. "Tell me more about Sophie."

"You'll meet her soon enough if you stop dawdling"

During their surprisingly long walk, Emily's attempts to draw out her friend continued to be unsuccessful. Vanessa batted away Emily's inquiries like a keen tennis player parrying volleys at the net. Changing the subject when Emily mentioned Sophie,

Vanessa chattered about her role as rescuer of her husband's ancestral home.

"Emily, I'm so glad you and Jack are coming for dinner this week. For one thing, I can't wait to meet Jack. And then I want you to see what I've done with Chillingworth Manor. It's quite transformed from the wreck I discovered when I met Nigel. You may think I just fell into the lap of luxury, but nothing could be further from the truth. The death duties and the sheer size of the property meant Nigel couldn't keep it up properly. After years of neglect, it was more than a bit crumbly. Nigel, poor lamb, had no idea what to do."

"You were able to set him straight, I imagine," Emily said hurrying to keep up with her friend's long strides.

"Indeed, I did. We now have a tearoom, a maze, pony rides, a falconer, and we are planning a ghost experience. The manor is a thriving tourist destination. All thanks to me."

Vanessa was no more modest than she had been as a small boastful girl, Emily observed. Sister Mary Margaret had often told her that the meek would inherit the earth, but Vanessa had taken no notice.

"Ah, we've arrived. And just on time." Vanessa glanced at her diamond watch.

On the corner across the street, the Union Jack flew above The Churchill Arms, a pub made festive by hanging baskets of flowers and ferns. Inside, Emily saw British flags, pennants, and memorabilia of Winston Churchill. Beer mugs and chamber pots hung above the bar. She moved closer to examine a large photo of the famous WWII prime minister and then walked along the wall, entranced by the photo montages from the 1940s. The pub was packed with people watching a soccer match on television and drinking beer.

"The Thai dining room has a totally different vibe than the pub's front room," Vanessa said. She spoke to the host, who led them to the back room where ferns and flowering tropical plants hung from the ceiling, creating a dense, jungle atmosphere.

"It's gorgeous," Emily said, looking around at the small room, crammed with greenery and blooming plants.

"So glad you could meet us today, Sophie!" Vanessa's voice boomed out in the small room as she rushed toward a thin, nondescript young woman, sitting at a small table by a row of pink cyclamen.

Sophie's eyes behind black-rimmed glasses darted around the room. "Yes, of course," she murmured, hunching her shoulders and lowering her head like a snail withdrawing into its shell.

Emily wondered why Vanessa was not more discreet if Sophie was in danger of immediate arrest.

Sophie had beige hair, pulled tightly back and gathered in a bun. She wore an oatmeal-colored twin set. Her face was pale and devoid of makeup, her eyes gray. Emily knew she would have a hard time recognizing this woman again, as nondescript as she was. She hoped the police would not quiz her if Sophie turned out to be a murderess.

"Sophie, I think Emily will be able to help you," Vanessa said in a loud whisper, leaning both hands on the table. "She's marvelous at getting to the crux of a matter. I know you haven't done anything wrong. Your tactics are never violent."

"No, of course not," Sophie murmured, not looking at Emily.

"What happened?" Vanessa lowered her voice and sat down. "Can you say? I know you pride yourself on keeping client information confidential, but you could be in serious trouble. Appearances, you know."

"Before I talk about this particular case, I think Emily deserves to know more about my services." Sophie squirmed in her seat. She looked as uncomfortable as a prelate at a wife-swapping party.

To Emily's surprise, Vanessa said. "Well, I'll leave you to it then," stood up and turned to leave.

"Wait, aren't you having lunch with us?" Emily called after her.

"Sophie will be more comfortable if your conversation is strictly *entre vous*. I can see that."

Emily wondered if Vanessa didn't want to risk being on hand when the police came barging in to arrest Sophie. But no, surely, she was being too suspicious of her friend.

"Please, join me," Sophie said in her soft voice. "We must order right away because there's a time limit. We have to finish our meal and be on our way in an hour."

Perhaps that was why this pub had been chosen. No time for awkward questions.

Emily perused the menu listing Thai food and settled on prawns and mushrooms with sticky rice. The food arrived quickly. "How delicious," Emily said after the first bite. My readers will definitely want to come here. Let me just jot down a few notes." Emily pulled out her red notebook:

> *Travelers' Tip: Don't miss The Churchill Arms. Devotees of the famous wartime prime minister will enjoy perusing memorabilia, photos, and patriotic flags while drinking Fuller Ale in this pub. Walk into the back room. You'll be surprised to find delicious Thai food served in a tropical garden. Wonderful shrimp and sticky rice. It's a delightful and unusual experience.*

"Forgive me," Emily said. "I'm a travel writer. I'm taking notes for my article."

"Yes, Vanessa told me all about you. She has great confidence in your abilities."

"She didn't tell me much about you at all. She said I had to hear what you do from your own lips. I did check out your website, Vindi Cat, but it was not very informative."

"No, it isn't meant to be." Sophie nabbed a prawn with her chopsticks.

"She did mention that you were somehow involved in the death of an MP who died of a snake bite." Emily looked expectantly at Sophie. "What happened?"

Sophie paused, scooped up a few grains of rice, then took a deep breath. "First, let me tell you how I came to start Vindi Cat. I own a temp agency that specializes in providing workers who have exceptionally strong computer skills. It has no connection to Vindi Cat. I stumbled into my side business purely by accident. My dear friend Angela (not her real name) came to me in tears. She told a familiar story of betrayal. She had been living with Clive for four years, confident that their relationship would end in marriage. When she found his computer carelessly left open and saw very explicit emails to another girl, she was devastated. Angela ended the relationship, but fury kept her awake at night.

"'I thought we were going to get married,' Angela told me. 'I wasted all that time and now I'll be too old to have a family. I know I should move on, but I can't seem to do it.'"

"'Of course, you can't,' I assured her. 'Your Clive's a bastard and deserves to be punished. Am I right?'"

"'Yes,' she said, 'but I have no way to punish him. He's moved on. He's deliriously happy. He's actually engaged…after telling me he just couldn't cope with commitment. I wish there was a way to make him suffer the way he makes me suffer.'

"'Perhaps there is...' I said. An idea had come to me. In fact, I easily found a way to hack into Clive's computer, discover emails to yet another girl and send them to his very wealthy fiancée the day after the wedding invitations went out. I posted some intimate photos on his Facebook page as well.

"Angela couldn't stop laughing. From then on, her sleep was untroubled. It was just a favor for a friend.

"Word began to spread. Angela made no secret of what I had done and didn't expect me to either. Soon I had a second business on my hands. I've been very clear that no physical harm can come to anyone. No violence. I just provide natural consequences for bad behavior."

"The unfaithful boyfriend certainly had it coming to him," Emily said. She couldn't help delighting in seeing the man's deceitfulness revealed, but Sophie's methods raised red flags in her law-abiding mind.

"I can see you're not convinced," said Sophie.

Emily realized—and not for the first time—that her thoughts were emblazoned for all to see as if a ticker tape were running across her forehead.

"I realize my service is unconventional," Sophie said. "I think of myself as providing mental health services, freeing people from their obsessions. I'd like you to meet one of my former clients. She'll tell you how much I helped her."

"I'd be happy to talk to your client, but I don't really understand the situation. How did you get involved in the murder?"

"It's not clear yet if there was a murder. A reporter running ahead of himself, I believe."

"Tell me what you think happened."

"Ah, I see our time is up." Sophie's shoulders sagged with relief.

The waiter was standing at their side with his bill in hand.

"The staff are very courteous, but they do need to turn over the tables fairly quickly to make a profit."

Hmm. Very convenient for Sophie to have their interview cut short. "So, what next?"

"One of my clients will contact you."

Back at the hotel, Emily found Jack in the palatial drawing room, typing at the computer. She put her hand on his shoulder. "You're not working, are you?"

Jack turned, a lock of black hair falling over his forehead. "Just checking up on a few of my patients. I wanted to call my *pro tem* but I felt so cramped in our tiny room and I'm afraid I'd violate patient confidentiality in here. How was your lunch?"

"Delicious. We had fabulous Thai food in the back room of a pub filled with Churchill memorabilia. Odd but delightful. I found out a bit more about Vindi Cat. Sophie told me how she got started trying to help people stop obsessing about wrongs they've suffered." Emily explained to Jack how Sophie had helped her friend Angela.

"Clive does sound like a bastard, but still it's a strange business," Jack said. "Did Sophie tell you how she was involved in the snake planting caper?"

"No. She claims that patient confidentiality prevents her from being more open with me. Apparently, she promises her clients she'll never repeat anything they tell her or reveal the nature of her services. Angela's story was an exception because she had spread the word far and wide herself. Sophie has arranged for me to meet one of her former clients who's willing to tell me more. I suspect that Sophie's activities may verge on illegal territory."

"Like the snakes."

"Probably."

"From what you've told me about your friend Vanessa, I had the impression she was a straight arrow who'd steer clear of anything illegal."

"She would. Especially since she doesn't want a hint of scandal to touch Nigel. But apparently Vanessa has a good reason to be grateful to Sophie. She isn't ready yet to tell me what it is. I think she wants me to approve of Sophie first."

"And do you?" Jack raised his eyebrow, an ability Emily envied.

"I'm reserving judgment."

Jack signed off on the computer, stood up and gave Emily a warm hug, then backed away at the sound of a voice speaking loudly in German. "Just be careful," he whispered, reluctantly letting her go. "I worry about you getting involved with this strange snake-wielding woman."

A heavy-set man in a tweed jacket and a girl, who was staring at her cell phone, walked into the room. He seemed to be scolding the child for not paying attention to him.

"We really must upgrade," Jack said.

"Okay," Emily agreed. "Let's talk to the front desk right now."

The young man at the desk, who looked very formal in a black suit and tie, spoke with a slight Eastern European accent. "Good afternoon, how can I assist you?"

"Is it possible to move to a larger room?" Jack asked. He helped himself to an apple in the bowl on the counter.

"Let me check for you." The clerk typed rapidly on the computer, which was out of sight below the ornate counter. "Alas. You already have the largest room in the hotel."

"Really?" Jack took a bite of the apple.

"Except for one."

"Is that one taken?"

"Well, no. It's Lily's room."

Emily wondered why he spoke as if they knew who Lily was, which was not the case.

"Would you care to see Lily's room?"

"Yes, please," Emily said, becoming more curious by the minute.

The young man led them to the elevator and up to the top floor. He swiped his passkey then flung the door open with a flourish.

Emily gasped. It was a sumptuous room. Sunlight streamed in through two windows that reached to the ceiling, illuminating white brocade wallpaper, gold silk drapes, and a marble fireplace. The four-poster bed with Corinthian columns was enormous. Through an open door Emily saw a white marble bathroom lit in a rosy glow by a recessed ceiling fixture. In the center of the room was a claw-foot tub, black as ebony.

"This is just one step up from our room?" Jack asked.

"The entire building was a gift to Lily Langtry from the Prince of Wales. This was her bedroom."

"Now, I see," Emily said. "How marvelous." She recalled that the actress Lily Langtry had been the mistress of Bertie, who later became King Edward VII in the 1870s. He was known for his romantic exploits. This explained the magnificence of the hotel's living room, dining room, bar and, of course, Lily's bedroom.

"What a generous guy," Jack said.

"A common trait of royalty," the clerk said, lowering his eyes. "The building is on the National Register and cannot be altered. Thus, our rooms are not as large as you would find in some chain hotels." He said the last two words with deep disdain. Clearly, he was proud of the hotel and its history and he was not going to suggest that it was a gift given for services rendered.

"Lily's room can sometimes be booked for a fairly modest sum, if done well in advance."

"But not for tonight, I assume."

"Oh no, I regret to say." He named a price well outside their travel budget.

Emily vowed to look online and find out more about Lily and Bertie. Her readers always wanted to hear the historical angle, or so she believed.

Chapter 3

The next evening, Emily and Jack arrived at the
gates of Chillingworth Manor in their rented Land
Rover. The estate was in the outskirts of Chipping
Campden, ninety miles from London, in the very heart
of the Cotswolds. Its location was convenient for
Emily, who planned to write about day trips from
London. Chipping Campden was her first stop.

After driving through a colonnade of plane trees,
they came upon a manor house of golden Cotswold
stone, draped in ivy, with turrets and mullioned
windows. As they pulled up in front of the house, a
uniformed man greeted them and offered to park their
car.

Vanessa, wearing a fresh, summery dress with a
fern-and-flower design, green on white, tripped down
the steps and hugged Emily with one arm. Her other
hand held a tall frosty glass garnished with a lime. "So
glad to see you! And, Jack, this is a pleasure. I'd like
you to meet my husband, Lord Nigel Chillingworth."
She gestured with her cocktail to a tall man with curly
ginger hair and a trim moustache, who stepped forward
and stuck out his hand.

"Pleased to meet you. Do come in," Nigel
stammered slightly. A huge gray dog that looked as if it
had been assembled from wire scraps kept to his side,
eying the newcomers with mournful suspicion.

"What kind of dog is that?" Jack asked. He reached
out his hand to pet it but something about its flattened

ears and bare fangs restrained him. "Some sort of hunting dog, I suppose."

"Yes, indeed, a Lurcher." Nigel smiled at Jack for the first time. "Name's Digger." He patted the huge beast.

"How lovely you look," Emily said to Vanessa.

"You are kind," Vanessa said. Her glossy brown hair hung just below her shoulders, curling slightly. "And you are as beautiful as ever, Emily. How I wish I were a blonde!"

Emily had missed the mutual praising and admiring that she and Vanessa had done since they were children. Such an important role for a best friend.

Nigel led the way through the marble-floored hallway, its walls hung with lethal-looking old weapons. "The Chillingworth family's armory," Nigel said, gesturing to the wall. "They were a blood thirsty lot if truth be told. Lots of swords, of course, broad swords and rapiers. I also have a mace, suitable for whapping an enemy over the head." Emily noted the sharp spikes on the head of the club and shuddered. "My favorite is the battle axe. It was ideal for close combat. It's still quite sharp."

"Nigel is proud of his family history, gory though it be," Vanessa said with an indulgent smile. "Chillingworth Manor has been in his family since the sixteenth century."

Dinner turned out to be lamb cutlets, mashed peas and new potatoes. "Delicious even if it didn't rise to the level of roast beef," Emily whispered later to Jack. They were served in a Jacobean wood-paneled dining room with a marble fireplace and portraits of self-satisfied ancestors in ornate frames.

"You've probably heard how I met my bride." Lord Chillingworth beamed at Vanessa down the length of the Chippendale dining table. "She was stumbling about in the greenery. I could hear bushes breaking and strangled cries. Then a tremendous thump. Digger began to bark like billy-o and took off as if he'd brought a fox to ground. He quickly found her writhing about in the grass, clutching her leg. Well, I had to haul the old bean off to the house and keep her there until she was on her pins again. It took several days to get her back in fighting trim and by that time I was smitten, well and truly smitten."

"They know that story, Nigel. I must say, you don't put the romantic spin on it that some men might."

"Just plain speaking. Tell them the facts." He bent his head and tucked into his lamb with gusto. Emily noticed an oasis of baldness among his tight curls.

"So, Vanessa, tell us more about this friend of yours," said Jack. "The one who is in some sort of trouble."

Emily wanted to kick him but the vastness if the table would not permit it. She wasn't sure how much Nigel knew and so she had been waiting for Vanessa to broach the subject.

"Ah," Vanessa cast a warning eye at her husband and pressed her lips together.

"You're not getting them involved in that dodgy business down in Chipping Campden, are you? A good man murdered and your friend very likely up to her neck in it."

"You don't know a thing about it, Nigel," Vanessa said.

"She is a damn fine-looking woman; I will say that for her. That long auburn hair and a bit of a come-hither glance, if you know what I mean." Nigel chuckled, not looking at Vanessa, who had put down her fork and was staring.

"You surprise me," Emily said. "Surely that isn't the same woman I met at the Churchill Arms." Emily thought of the timid English matron with sallow skin and thick glasses.

"Sophie has a background in theatre," Vanessa said. "She enjoys varying her appearance. I believe it comes in very handy in her line of work."

Emily was growing more curious by the minute.

"Of course, I don't know that fellow who was killed," Nigel said. "Still, it's a god-awful way to die. Bitten by serpents. Not sporting. It probably was a woman. Cleopatra and the asp come to mind."

"Nonsense," Vanessa snapped. "I refer you to 'The Speckled Band'."

"Haw! Got me there, m'dear."

Emily recognized one of her favorite Sherlock Holmes stories featuring a snake that had been trained to slither down a bell pull dangling by a bed and inject its venom into a hapless maiden. Holmes' killer was a man, one who knew how to charm a snake.

After dinner, Nigel took Jack aside and suggested a brandy in the library. "After that drive down from London, you need another little pick-me-up."

Jack looked at Emily, clearly wondering how she felt about being left out of the invitation.

Emily nodded encouragement at him. "Vanessa and I are going to take a turn in the garden." Emily hoped she'd find out more if she was alone with Vanessa.

"Since you've been kind enough to invite us to stay the night, Lord Chillingworth, I'd be glad to have a snifter," Jack said.

"Well done, old man. And do call me Nigel."

Digger kept close to Nigel's heels as they headed for the library.

Emily followed Vanessa down the hall, through the orangery and out French doors into the garden. On one side of the broad pathway was a formal rose garden with a fountain and on the other side a maze. Vanessa led Emily into the maze where the high boxwood hedge completely enclosed them in greenery.

"I'm glad I finally had a chance to meet your husband," Emily said. "What a nice man."

"He is. But Nigel's not easy to get to know. He sometimes overdoes his old English squire routine. It's as if he's auditioning for a part in some community theatre production. Just his shyness really."

Emily followed Vanessa as she walked quickly without hesitation deep into the winding maze, weaving her way along the narrow path that forced them to walk single file. "How do you find your way through here?"

"Practice. Besides there is a clue. Every now and then you can find a little bent branch like this one bound with red thread that shows you which way to turn." Vanessa paused to show Emily the tiny marker.

"I would not like to try it on my own." The greenery, which reached far above her head, seemed to be closing in on her. Emily was glad when they reached the center of the maze where an ornate gazebo of white filigree ironwork was encircled by a tall flowering hedge.

"My hideaway," Vanessa said. "Come inside."

Inside the gazebo were wicker chairs with blue and white cushions, and a glass-topped table set with two wine glasses. "Now we can chat in comfort." Vanessa opened a small fridge disguised as a wicker hamper and pulled out a bottle of white wine. She plopped a strawberry into each glass and poured.

"A grownup version of our old clubhouse in the hollow tree," Emily said with delight.

"Yes. I thought of that." Vanessa raised her glass. "Here's to you and Jack! I do like him, Emily. I think you'll be very happy. When is the wedding?"

"Oh no rush."

Vanessa raised an eyebrow. "Most brides are chomping at the bit."

Emily didn't know how to respond so she didn't. She changed the subject. "Tell me how you came to be such good friends with Sophie. She must have helped you in some extraordinary way for you to be so loyal to her."

"You're right, of course. I owe her a great deal."

"How so?"

"Oh, Emily, a year ago I was consumed with anger. You remember my father?"

Emily nodded. She had a vague memory of a quiet man with a gentle smile, reading a magazine by the fireside. She had spent a lot of time at Vanessa's house when she was a girl but had not paid much attention to her father.

"Then you know how kind and hardworking he was. When I was at the U, he discovered a kind of valve or gadget of some sort that turned out to be useful in heart operations. He was an assistant in a medical device company. Everyone there knew how handy he was at fixing things. Well, a gizmo he came up with became the basis of a very important invention for the company. George Mogg was credited with developing it. He never gave my father credit, much less let him profit from it. Even worse, he fired my father because he was afraid he would somehow manage to hog the spotlight. Quite the last thing my father would do. But he did expect fair dealings. I wanted my father to sue and demand justice. He refused, didn't want the fuss. He fell into a dark depression.

So, without telling my dad, I went to Mogg's office and confronted the dreadful man. As you can imagine, my knees were knocking. He's quite intimidating and I was just a girl. But I told Mogg I thought he owed my father gratitude and compensation, that it was just evil to have fired him. After all, he made the discovery.

Mogg smirked. 'It's just business. If you're smart, you win. If not, you lose.'

"My father died soon afterward. I blamed Mogg.

"Mogg has been on television boasting that the rich deserve their good life because they're smarter and work harder than the poor. He is well known to believe that anyone who is homeless or on welfare is stupid and lazy. The last straw came when he decided to run for Congress."

"What a horrible man. You must have been furious."

"Well, yes, I was. But that's the beauty part of Vindi Cat. My anger's gone."

"How? Therapy? Hypnosis?"

"Oh no. Revenge. Sweet revenge."

"What did you do?"

"I didn't have to do a thing. I had heard from a friend about Sophie's service, Vindi Cat. Sophie is uniquely situated to succeed in the business of revenge. As she may have told you, she runs a temp agency whose staff has strong computer skills. It gives her an entrée to many organizations and computer systems. All this was useful in her new venture—helping women who have been wronged.

"Yes, Sophie told me about Angela. What did she do to relieve *you* of your anger?"

"I'll let Sophie tell you herself. She really deserves all the credit. We're sworn to secrecy. I'd be struck by lightning if I told you her methods after I made so many promises. You probably remember your Latin, so I don't need to tell you the significance of her website's name."

Emily had let every bit of Latin slide from her memory, so she waited for Vanessa to elaborate.

"Vindicata. She avenges."

"Ahh, yes, I see."

"Sophie said I would hear from one of her former clients but so far no word," Emily said.

"Sophie gave me a message for you. She knew you were staying here tonight so she thought it would be convenient if you met her in Chipping Campden tomorrow. She wants to introduce you to one of her clients who has volunteered to talk about her experience. I told her you would be staying at The Noel Arms in the center of town."

"I'll wait to hear from her at the hotel."

"We had better get back. It's starting to get dark."

Emily took her last sip of wine and stood up.

"There's a secret exit at the back of the maze so we don't have to wend our way back through the maze as darkness falls." Vanessa pushed against a vine covered door behind the gazebo that would be invisible unless one knew where to look. Emily ducked down to follow her.

Beyond the maze, Emily saw a hill descending to stables and green fields reaching far into the distance. "Oh, it's breathtaking," Emily said. "The manor, the garden, all of it."

"I must admit I'm quite proud. You should have seen it two years ago. The garden overgrown with weeds. The roof leaking. Buckets in the hallways."

"Nigel must be very grateful to you."

"Oh, he is. His family has owned Chillingworth Manor for more than four hundred years and it means the world to him. Over there you can see the pony yard and children's play area. School groups come through every week. Nigel gives the tours himself. He's quite good at it. You should hear him describe the English Civil War. His family was adept at switching sides at just the right times so they never lost their land."

Twilight was deepening the shadows. "Let's turn back," Vanessa said, leading the way along the flagstone path that ran between the maze and the formal rose garden. "The fountain with its spouting maidens and gargoyles has always been here but the rose bushes had all died off. I worked with a landscape expert to restore the garden. Up ahead you can see the orangery where we serve tea on weekends."

That evening, Emily called her mother and told her about her visit to Vanessa and her husband, Nigel. "Right now, I'm lounging on an enormous four-poster bed in one of Vanessa's guest rooms with a fireplace and a full suit of armor."

"How marvelous. Vanessa was always such a nice little girl. Is her home really very grand or was she exaggerating when she wrote to you?"

"It's fabulous. A manor house with turrets, a formal garden and a maze. You'd love it. I'll email you photos."

"You know I can never open up those little attachments."

"Sure, you can. Fanny will help."

Her mother sniffed. "If your sister ever comes over here. Aren't you going to ask about Stanley?" She was dog sitting for Emily and Jack's Golden Retriever.

"How is Stanley?" Emily assumed he was being spoiled so there was no need to ask.

"Despondent. I'm signing him up for agility training to take his mind off missing you."

"Good heavens. You don't have to be agile yourself, do you? You know how you tip over."

"Nonsense. We'll make a good team"

Emily didn't want to encourage her. If she paid no attention, maybe her mother would forget this mad idea. "I have to go now, Mom."

"Don't be in such a hurry. How's Jack? Have you two set the wedding date yet?"

"We're a little busy right now. I'm working on my article and Jack on his." She didn't mention the murder investigation. "We're not even thinking about our wedding."

"Well, you should be. I talked to Father Cronin and the church is already booked well into the summer."

"It will be fine. Don't worry."

"Maybe you could be married at Vivian's castle or whatever it is. Destination weddings are all the rage."

"No. Not happening."

"You don't have to be so testy, Emily. I'm just trying to help you."

Emily reassured her mother of her undying gratitude and rang off.

She turned to Jack who was sprawled on the bed, scrolling through his phone. "My mother is applying the thumb screws. She wants to start planning our wedding."

"It's *our* wedding, remember? Don't let her get to you. Whatever you like will be fine. Come here." He grinned at her and reached out to pull her down beside him.

Emily realized once again that she had definitely picked the right guy.

The next day, after a hearty English breakfast, Jack and Emily drove a few miles into Chipping Campden where golden stone buildings lined the High Street and an ancient market hall occupied the center of town. "I love it," Emily said, beaming with happiness. "A typical old-fashioned British village. I feel as if we've stumbled into an episode of *Midsummer Murders*." They checked in at The Noel Arms, a handsome building with a red-and-gold coat of arms and hanging baskets of red begonias by the door. The clerk at the front desk handed Emily an envelope. "This message arrived for you madam." She tucked it in her pocket. Their room was large, bright and airy with a king-sized bed and a huge bathroom with a shower and two sinks. Jack was delighted. Emily opened the envelope and read. "Please meet me in the pub at The Noel Arms at 4 p.m."

"Will you mind if I abandon you and meet Sophie this afternoon?" Emily handed Jack her message.

"Not at all. It works out perfectly. I have to work on my article." Jack had assembled the research and now had to organize and edit his article, "The Long-Term Effects of Childhood Abuse and Trauma on Chronic Illnesses in Adults." He planned to submit his article to the state medical journal. "Then I have a nap scheduled." Jack's years as a medical resident left him with a permanent sleep deficiency so he grabbed any opportunity for a quick snooze.

Promptly at four, Emily walked downstairs to the pub, conveniently located in the hotel. It was a convivial gathering place with brick walls, timber beams and a large fireplace. Men and women, several of them with their dogs beside them, were clustered around the bar.

Emily saw two women at a table by the fireplace but didn't recognize either one. Then she remembered Sophie's penchant for disguise and looked more closely. Sophie's hair was pulled back and she wore a tweed jacket, long skirt and sensible hiking shoes. A heather wool scarf was wound about her neck. At her feet lay a brown and white spaniel with muddy paws.

Sophie looked up and smiled. "Ah here you are, Emily. I'd like you to meet one of my former clients. Eunice has kindly agreed to tell you how I helped her."

Emily was startled by Eunice's plainness and immediately felt guilty, so she greeted her with excessive warmth. The woman's small eyes were close together, crowding her formidable nose, her chin receded, merging with her neck. She wore no makeup. Like Sophie, Eunice was dressed in warm tweeds, hers an unflattering blend of purple and orange. She greeted Emily without smiling. Her face gave nothing away.

The dog opened one eye and thumped its tail. Emily wondered if it was really Sophie's pet or a prop of some kind.

"Eunice is a friend of Angela's. You remember I told you how I got started helping Angela to achieve closure after her boyfriend betrayed her?"

"Yes, of course."

"Eunice was impressed by my success and wanted to hire me to perform a similar service for her. She had a particularly obnoxious and hypocritical boss who treated her badly. The injustice of it tormented her. How could I say no?"

Eunice leaned forward and nodded, apparently eager to tell her tale. "Yes, yes. My boss, Mr. Conley, flattered people to an extent that would make a normal person physically ill, but the board lapped it up." She jutted her head in and out like a bird as she spoke. I said to Sophie: 'If only they could hear how he talks about them behind their backs!'"

"Perhaps that can be arranged, I told her," Sophie said.

"At the next board meeting," Eunice continued, "my boss started up his PowerPoint presentation with a lush audio component. There was a rush of triumphant music, a video of the CEO shaking hands with the chair of the board. The voice-over rang out: 'Flinders is an idiot. Doesn't know what he's talking about.' There was a disturbed murmur in the room. Whispers hissed. "That's Conley's voice isn't it? Yes. Yes, I'm sure it is." Heads craned around looking for him. Now on the screen, our company's lead spokesperson stood at a podium, but the voice-over was Conley's. 'Why doesn't he just stick to the goddam script? The man's an idiot.'

"By the time my boss managed to turn off the video, the damage had been done. In a few minutes, he was packing up his belongings while a security guard stood by, ready to escort him out of the office."

Eunice chortled with delight. "Sophie had preserved the whole episode on video and, in fact, shared it on the company's Facebook page so all the members of the company could enjoy it. I slept easily in my bed that night for the first time in weeks."

"Nobody thought of the lowly temp worker who was assisting with the presentation," Sophie said. "As my reputation for results spread, my clients became more numerous. And my rates rose accordingly."

Emily wondered why Eunice had been so incensed by her boss's hypocrisy, a trait that was not especially rare. "Your boss does sound like a dreadful man. But why did it affect you so much? Surely, he's not alone in being two-faced. Losing his job seems a harsh penalty."

Sophie looked at Eunice. "Do you want to tell her? You don't have to, of course."

Eunice took a deep breath and pursed her lips as if ready to spit out a lemon seed. Deep lines around her mouth suggested it was her default expression.

"That's not the whole story. His hypocrisy was simply a way to nail him. I had been in my position for three years and had received excellent performance evaluations. So, when my immediate boss quit I was confident I'd be promoted." She clenched her jaw.

Emily doubted if all Eunice's rage had dissipated as she claimed. "But you were not," Emily encouraged her.

"No. A very pretty young woman had recently been hired. I don't say she was incompetent exactly, but she was definitely at the beginning of a rather steep learning curve. Mr. Conley would perch his large buttocks on the corner of her desk, beam at her and chat away about this and that. He had never passed the time of day with me in three years. Oh no. All business he was. But little Gwennie was a different story." Eunice took a sip of cider and squared her shoulders.

"Let me guess. Gwennie was promoted over you. Did you ever challenge him about it?"

Eunice gave a hollow laugh. "I tried. He never seemed to have time to discuss it in any detail. He muttered that Gwen was a better 'fit' with our company's image. I was so angry I quit. Gave two weeks' notice. Mr. Conley looked relieved. I should have just walked out on the spot but then I would have missed all the fun. I wouldn't have been there when he received his comeuppance." She smiled at Sophie. "Before Sophie helped me, I used to lie awake at night dreaming of revenge. I fantasized about shrieking insults, punching him, stabbing him. Finally, I settled on shooting him in the groin as most appropriate, not really planning to do it, but daydreaming about it. Then I heard Angela's story and saw a less drastic alternative."

"My methods are never violent," Sophie said.

Eunice nodded. "But he had to be punished. You can see that. His hypocrisy and general loathsomeness as a human being gave Sophie all the ammunition she needed."

Both women were looking expectantly at Emily as if waiting for absolution. Even the spaniel lifted its head and gazed at her with interest.

"Wow. What a tale." Emily could see how Sophie's business could land her in deep trouble.

Later, as she and Jack walked through the village of Chipping Campden, Emily told him Eunice's story. "I couldn't help cheering at the way Sophie exposed Conley's hypocrisy. He sounds like a horrible man."

"But we've only heard Eunice's version."

"True. And nobody would care to see every comment they'd ever made displayed for all the world to see."

"God, no."

"Eunice seemed consumed by anger, tormented by thoughts of revenge. As she was speaking, I thought of all the news reports about disgruntled employees who go on shooting sprees and mow down their former colleagues. I could see Eunice doing that after brooding and obsessing for a year or two."

"That only happens in the U.S. where it's so easy to get a gun, even for the clearly deranged."

"Still, Sophie may be offering an alternative to violence. She certainly thinks that's the case. She still hasn't told me if she was involved in the MP's death, but it no longer seems preposterous to think that she planted the snakes."

"She assigns herself the roles of judge and jury."

"She doesn't judge at all. She just accepts her friends' versions of events without question."

"Hmm." Jack sounded like a physician about to impart bad news to his patient. "Did you find out what she did to the MP?" he asked.

"No. Nor did I find out why Vanessa thinks Sophie will be arrested. Despite her fears, apparently no one has connected Sophie with the MP's death. According to the latest newspaper report, the snakes were not poisonous and so far, the coroner has not named a cause of death. So even if Sophie did plant the snakes, which is far from certain, they couldn't have killed him. Or could they? Could Edward have died of fright?"

"Possibly. We've all heard about the placebo effect, how people who take a pill with no medical value can really be cured if they believe in it."

"The power of faith."

"Yes, but there's an opposite effect that's less well known. The decebo effect. If someone believes that something will kill them, it very well might. People who are told they have a deadly disease, sometimes die of it before there's any real physical damage. The mind can have a powerful effect. Sometimes an autopsy doesn't even show a cause of death in such cases."

"So, if Edward believed that the snakes could kill him, he might have died of fright? Even if the snakes weren't poisonous? Even if he didn't have a heart condition?"

"Yes, it is possible."

"It would be hard to convict Sophie for a prank if she couldn't have foreseen the result."

"That's a question for a lawyer. If a malicious prank leads to death, does it matter if the perpetrator knew how deadly it could be? The aim was to harm."

Chapter 4

To her horrible surprise, Emily awoke to a winter
wonderland. She looked out the window to see that
several inches of snow had fallen, and the sky was an
ominous leaden gray. Her plan to write about walking
through the Cotswolds in glorious springtime seemed
doomed. Starting with Chipping Campden, she was
going to visit several of the charming villages in the
Cotswold Hills, a 25 by 90 mile area of
Gloucestershire, famous for its beautiful countryside
and quaint inns and pubs. Only a couple of hours drive
from London, the Cotswold villages were a perfect
destination for tourists who wanted to experience the
joys of rural England.

"My readers do not want to learn about hiking
through the snow," Emily said. "They expect sunshine,
crocuses, daffodils, and birdsong."

"Now you see why the poet Browning specified
April," Jack said, putting his arms around her.

"Don't rub it in. England is usually lovely in March.
This happens to be an exception."

"We'll make the best of it. No need to rush off to
breakfast." He pulled her closer.

Emily saw the wisdom of his advice.

Presently, Emily and Jack went downstairs and sat at
a table in the lovely formal dining room with white and
lavender striped wallpaper, white beams and a
fireplace. They helped themselves to orange juice,
pineapple, strawberries and croissants from the buffet in
the center of the room. Staff brought them coffee and

took their order for their full English breakfast: fluffy scrambled eggs, sausage, ham, grilled tomatoes, black pudding, fried bread, and beans. They lingered over their enormous feast because there was no need to rush on such an inclement day.

Finally, unable to eat any more, they decided to explore the town. As they passed the front desk, Jack asked for a newspaper.

"Oh no, sir. Not in this weather. It would be impossible. You're lucky you don't have to leave town this morning. Many of our guests are stranded. The trains aren't going anywhere; airplanes are grounded; taxis won't venture out. We're basically snowed in."

"Really?"

Emily was as astonished as Jack. She supposed that the snow must have picked up quite a bit since she last looked out the window. But when she opened the door, she discovered the sidewalk was covered with just a couple of inches of sleet.

"There's only an inch or two of snow on the ground," Jack said. "Why are the Brits reacting as if it were a blizzard? At home, we wouldn't turn a hair."

"Minnesota is well equipped to deal with snow. Here they don't even have snow shovels. Hence the looks of horrified alarm and the icy walks."

Jack sighed. "Well, let's carry on." He and Emily walked down the High street, which extended for only five or six blocks in this very small town. Emily discovered that the shops she wanted to visit were closed so she suggested exploring the area just outside of town. They turned down a side street and soon found themselves heading into the countryside. The dirt path was alarmingly icy and slippery. Daffodils were plastered flat against the frosted grass.

Cold was seeping up from the soles of her shoes so when her phone rang, Emily was glad of an excuse to stop. She heard Vanessa's anxious voice. "Just as I feared, Emily. The police have received an anonymous letter accusing Sophie of murder. It's all over the news. You must have seen it."

"No. It was snowing this morning, so we didn't get a paper. Tell me more."

Vanessa read aloud. "An anonymous source has named a woman who, the letter claims, was involved in the death of Edward Westley. The letter says that the snakes were maliciously introduced into his bedroom to cause a heart attack in a man who was known to be terrified of them. This paper will not name the suspect until she is charged. Currently, police are seeking her help in their inquiries."

"Oh, dear. I just met Sophie and heard from one of her grateful clients."

"She's impressive, isn't she?"

"An interesting woman definitely. I still want to hear how she helped you."

"Let's meet for tea at Badger's Hall Tea Room. You'll love it. Nigel wants to take Jack tramping across the fields. It will be muddy and unpleasant, but Digger will adore it. Does Jack like hiking?"

"We both do actually." Emily recalled her plan of hiking through sunny green meadows where sheep grazed, and flowers bloomed.

"Well, you wouldn't want to hike on such a nasty day. Shall we say three in the afternoon at Badger's Hall? It's on the High Street in Chipping Campden, very handy for you."

When Emily saw the sign with a dapper badger, a cup of tea in hand, marking the entrance to Badger's Hall she thought of *The Wind in the Willows* a favorite when she was a child and knew she was going to like this place. She pushed open the door and to her surprise saw Sophie as well as Vanessa waiting for her inside the snug tearoom with beamed ceilings. Sophie had not altered her appearance this time and was still clad in tweeds.

Emily wanted to ask her if she was going to turn herself in or go on the lam, but she restrained herself.

"I did want Sophie to tell you what she did for me before she goes to the police. I want you to understand why I'm so grateful."

"I can't imagine who the malicious letter writer was," Sophie said, "but the MP certainly didn't have a horror of snakes. Far from it."

She sounded sure of herself, but Emily noticed a slight tremor in her hands and wondered if doubt was creeping in.

"Are you going to the police?" Emily asked. "So, you can answer their questions and clear up any misunderstanding?"

"I regret that isn't possible," Sophie said. "Answering police questions would violate my oath of secrecy. Unfortunately, my specialty is so unusual that the right of client confidentiality is not recognized."

"That's why I've been so worried," Vanessa said. "I knew Sophie wouldn't say anything."

"Can you ask your client to come forward and explain to the police?" Emily asked.

Sophie looked uncomfortable. Her eyes darted away, and she began to fiddle with her tweed scarf.

"Let's order the afternoon tea," Vanessa said brightly. "Shall we start with a flute of prosecco? It has such a reviving effect in times of trouble."

Emily was quick to agree. A waiter soon brought a three-tiered tea tray of tiny quiches, sausage rolls, cucumber sandwiches, prawn sandwiches, eclairs, slices of cake, currant scones with jam and clotted cream, and frosted brownies. Emily quickly whipped out her red notebook.

> *Travelers' Tip:* Lovely as teatime is in London, you may find it even more delightful in the countryside. Don't miss Afternoon Tea at Badger's Hall Tea Room in Chipping Campden. Be sure to arrive very hungry.

As they nibbled treats and sipped the house tea, which Emily found a little milder than her favorite Assam and very flavorful, Vanessa said, "As I told you, I couldn't get over my anger at the way George Mogg treated my father. Nigel told me to forget it, that I had left all that behind me in the States. But I just couldn't. I had nightmares of revenge.

"Then Eunice told me her story and I was quite impressed."

Emily noticed that despite all the promise of secrecy, word got around in no time.

Vanessa apparently realized what Emily was thinking. "Oh, Eunice didn't tell me the details, or who was targeted, but she did tell me the marvelous effect it had on her. She was devastated when she lost her job. Now she's perfectly happy. She started over at a firm that really appreciates her.

"I wanted the same results for myself. I knew I had a chance to get back at Mogg. He was coming to a conference in the UK and would be here for several days. I went to Sophie and begged and beseeched her to find a way to get even."

"It was just a matter of revealing his true character," Sophie said. "I gave him opportunities to hoist himself by his own petard, as it were. This is a fairly long story as it was one of my most complex and successful efforts." Sophie did look pleased with herself. "Are you sure you want to hear it?"

"Yes, yes, please go on." Emily bit into an éclair.

"George was staying at a posh hotel in London, which shall remain nameless, during a business conference. He was regular in his habits, which was a tremendous help to me," Sophie said. "George began each day with a vigorous workout in the hotel exercise room, followed by a shower in his own room. His sweatpants had no pockets so, on the day I planned my action, he left his phone and wallet in his room and took only his key card. Sophie continued to tell how she had wreaked revenge on George.

George Mogg's Story

Since the conference had ended, George had packed the night before. He planned to exercise, shower, eat breakfast, check out and catch a taxi to the airport, then back to Minneapolis.

Supremely pleased with the result of his business dealings, he hummed as he strode to the exercise room. After an hour on the machines, he was ready for the day.

When he thrust his key card into the slot, however, a red light flashed, denying him entry. He tried several more times, then pounded on the door in frustration, as if some minion inside could open the door. Sadly for him, that was not the case. Muttering under his breath, he went down to the lobby and slapped his card on the desk.

"Give me a card that works, goddammit! This is a piece of shit."

"I'm sorry, sir. What is your name?"

"George V. Moggs." George rapped his fingers on the desk while the clerk typed rapidly, his eyes darting back and forth across the screen.

"What the hell's taking so long?"

"I can't seem to find your name in our system, sir."

"Well, goddammit, call over someone who can." George looked at the clerk's nametag and read out, "Delmaaar," drawing it out as if his name was somehow ridiculous. "Where the hell's your supervisor, Delmaar?"

His raised voice had already drawn the attention of the supervisor, who sidled up beside Delmar and asked George, "Is there a problem, sir?"

"There sure as hell is!" George repeated his demand for a proper key card in a louder voice.

The supervisor tried his luck at the computer with the same result.

"According to our system, you're not a guest here."

"Damn it. I'm staying in room 433. I've been staying at this hotel for four days. Of course, I'm in the system." George turned to Delmar. "You've seen me before. We've spoken." He had found reason to correct Delmar often enough that he expected to be remembered.

"I don't recall, sir." Delmar's face was blank. In fact, he probably recalled George's rudeness very well.

"Perhaps you've confused our hotel with another," his supervisor suggested.

"I was in your goddam exercise room. Just open the door to 433 for me. All my bags are there. This is ridiculous. Goddam incompetents."

The supervisor sighed. "We are going well beyond what is required to accommodate you, sir, so please lower your voice. You are disturbing our guests."

The supervisor escorted a furious, fuming George Moggs to Room 433 and opened the door. The room was empty, the bed neatly made.

George was stunned. "Perhaps I remembered my room number wrong." It was a huge concession. He never admitted to being wrong.

Back in the lobby, he turned to Delmar. "Try the goddam computer again. I might have the room number wrong, but you know I've been staying here. You've seen me. We've spoken."

Delmar shook his head. These conversations had been so one-sided and unpleasant that George did not believe that Delmar could possibly have forgotten them. George began to swear.

Two security officers gently took him under each arm and escorted him out the elaborate brass doors. "Please don't return, sir," the supervisor said. "Your intemperate language and your appearance reflect poorly on our hotel. If you do come back, I'll be forced to summon the police."

George stood in the sunshine, baffled and enraged. He had no money, no ID, no way of catching his flight. He had never felt so helpless.

The idiot supervisor had mentioned his appearance as if he looked like a bum. George realized that, through no fault of his own, he wasn't looking particularly dapper. Of course, he hadn't shaved. That ritual followed his exercise routine. In fact, he was sweaty, unshaven, and wearing exercise clothes barely fit for the gym.

He wanted his breakfast—black coffee, grapefruit, muesli and a poached egg—but didn't even have enough money to buy a cup of coffee.

George stopped at a shop where the smell of hot coffee and pastries was overpowering. His mouth began to water. He asked the muscular, grumpy man at the counter if he could use his phone. It was an emergency.

"Okay but make it quick."

George called his PA's number and instead of Deirdre's reassuring voice heard a strange woman say, "McLeod, Mogg, and Smith, Ethel speaking."

"Who the hell are you?" George barked. "I want to speak to Deirdre."

"I'm sorry, sir, she's on sick leave today. I'm the temp."

He gave a huge sigh, suggesting Ethel was somehow responsible for Deirdre's absence and possibly his other woes as well. "Well put me through to Angus then."

"Mr. McLeod is not available at this particular moment in time."

"It's urgent. If he's in a meeting, interrupt him. Tell him it's George Mogg. I have to speak to him right away."

"Oh dear, Mr. Morgan, I regret that Mr. McLeod is not available."

"Mogg, not Morgan. Are you deaf?" Seething, George demanded to be put through to voice mail.

"Certainly, Mr. Miggins."

"Mogg, goddam it. Can't you get anything right?

There was a series of clicks. "Oh, my goodness, I wonder if this is the right button."

The connection ended.

"I need to try again," George said, clinging to the receiver, which the clerk was now trying to pry from his hand.

"Not on this phone, mate. We're a shop here, not a bloody media center."

George cursed at him and ironically enough plotted to exact revenge. He would see the hotel flunky and the manager fired and then somehow punish this man who was slamming down the receiver and glowering at him. Heads would roll, he vowed.

As he turned away, his mutterings began to attract attention. He knew he was not looking his best. Hunger pangs gnawed more insistently. He could hear loud protesting gurgles from his empty stomach. The smell of beef and onions was tantalizing. He didn't want breakfast anymore. He wanted a huge lunch. A hamburger, potato salad, a dill pickle, coleslaw on the side.

His flight would be boarding now. He was going to miss an international flight. "Dammit, dammit," he muttered as he left the shop.

Baffled in his attempts to reach his office, he turned to a less appealing prospect—his ex-wife Agatha. He found a gift shop and pleaded an emergency, he had to reach his wife. The store smelled of perfumed candles, but thank god, no torturing food aromas. The woman at the counter sniffed once or twice and looked him up and down with disfavor.

"Our phone is just for business, not for customers. Customers have their cell phones, don't they? Except for the homeless."

"I'm not homeless. I just need to make a call. Look, when I get this mess sorted out, I'll pay you ten pounds. Twenty."

She hooted. "When you get it sorted out, I'll be dead and singing in the heavenly choir. Well, I suppose we must have pity on those less fortunate. I'll let you make a call but make it quick."

He gritted his teeth and dialed Agatha's number. Her cheery recorded voice answered. "Hi, there, I'm on vacation, no use at all leaving me a message. Try back in a week or two. Ta ta. Kisses."

How many times had he told her not to leave a message saying she would be out of town? She might as well put out a sign that said, "Welcome, burglars. Help yourself." Stupid bitch. Thieves were probably hauling out her valuables and loading them into their van right now. He slammed down the phone.

"There's a Homeless Center down the road. You might try there. A hot meal will do you a world of good. But you'd better hustle. They run out pretty quick."

"I'm not homeless, goddamit."

Apparently, she thought she'd secured her place in heaven with her suggestion for she beamed at him with kindly pity. "Of course not. Still."

"Thank you," George muttered gracelessly as he headed out the door.

It was starting to drizzle, and the wind had picked up. His sweaty exercise clothes felt damp and chill as they clung to his body. He'd probably catch pneumonia. The hotel would pay, oh, yes, they would pay for this.

Despite his churlish response to the clerk's suggestion, George found himself walking in the direction she had pointed. He wandered into a much less prosperous part of town where a line of scruffy looking, unshaven men was standing along the side of a small concrete building, apparently waiting for the door to open. He fell into line.

Presently, a burly man pushed him aside and growled, "My mate was saving me a spot here. Get away." George thought he had reached the point where his heart might burst with fury. He pushed back and yelled, "I was here first. Wait your turn!." But the other man was much stronger and easily pushed him aside and took his place. "If they run out, it's not me that's going hungry."

In fact, when the door opened, both men managed to get a bowl of soup and a slice of bread. George, known for his discerning palate, fell upon his meal and slurped it down as fast as he could, half afraid someone would snatch it from him.

He spent the afternoon going from shop to shop for warmth, moving on when he felt too conspicuous. As it began to grow dark, he felt exhausted. He walked until he came to a bridge and climbed down the embankment. It was warmer underneath the bridge and he could hear cars roaring overhead, a soothing white noise. He curled up against the concrete and fell asleep. Soon he was shaken awake.

"Hey what do you think you're doing? This is my place. Get away from here."

George was pulled to his feet by a stringy old man with wild eyes and gray hair that stood on end. "Find your own spot."

George hadn't the strength to contend with this apparently crazy person. He probably had a knife. He walked to the end of the overpass, noting that men slept all along its length.

A voice called out to him. "Hey." He looked down at a middle-aged woman with a bundle of clothes beside her. "You might find a place to sleep at St. Crispin's. You go just up the street there and turn right."

"Why don't you go there?' George uncharacteristically wondered about the welfare of someone besides his own dear self.

"I have my regular place; my friends bunk here. When it's really cold I do go to St. Crispin's. Good luck."

That night he slept in a large auditorium on a pallet. The noise of snorting and grunting, the smell of unwashed bodies assaulted his senses. But eventually sheer exhaustion and misery took their toll. He slept until morning.

He walked out into a clear bright day, hungrier and more miserable than he had ever been in his life. He passed a food shop and went inside. It smelled wonderful. He sidled along until he reached a refrigerated counter and reached down for a sandwich.

He pulled it under his sweatshirt and hurried for the exit.

A buzzer sounded and the clerk yelled, "Stop where you are!"

A police officer wandered over from the next aisle. "Right, mate, put your hands behind your back."

"I'll put it back." George started to reach under his shirt for the sandwich.

The officer yelled, "Freeze! Hands where I can see them."

George put up his hands. The sandwich dropped to his feet.

"Hands behind your back." The officer cuffed him.

"You can't arrest me for just a sandwich."

"Sure, I can, mate. Petty theft."

The clerk said, "Thanks, officer. This is the sixth time I've been robbed this week. It doesn't seem like much, but it adds up. I don't make much of a profit anyway."

George wondered if the clerk felt a bit guilty for sending a man to jail for stealing something so small.

"He deserves it!" The man yelled after them. "Lock him up. Throw away the key."

Well, that cleared up that question. No guilt at all.

Although George thought he had truly entered hell and would soon find himself in a jail cell with serial killers, his arrest turned out to be the best thing that had happened in a quite a while. He was allowed to contact his lawyer who managed to get charges dropped and wired him money. His lawyer also contacted the hotel on his behalf, and he was able to report that the hotel had recovered its information about him, and he was definitely still registered there.

George would have been glad never to set foot in the hotel again, but all his belongings were there. A police officer drove him to the hotel where he was welcomed by the supervisor who had treated him so outrageously the day before.

"Your lawyer has contacted me, and we have straightened out the very understandable confusion. In fact, your room is not 433 but 333. You were mistaken and unfortunately our system was experiencing a minor glitch at that time that prevented us from being able to correct your error."

George wanted to grab him by the throat and squeeze hard, but even more than that he wanted a hot shower, his own clothes, his billfold, identification and money. He kept quiet, biting down on his knuckle, as he rode up to the third floor with the supervisor, prattling beside him about how unfortunate and yet perfectly understandable and completely Mr. Mogg's own fault it was.

"It's too bad you didn't remember your room number because then the confusion would have been resolved very quickly. I always recommend writing the number down on a bit of paper." The supervisor stood helpfully beside him as George inserted the key card and saw the reassuring green light flash. He opened the door and his room was just as he had left it. He had been so sure of the number. He never made mistakes like that. He was a numbers guy.

George thought his troubles were at an end. His shower was as soothing and warm as he had dreamed it would be. His huge meal of steak and baked potato, salad and red wine was indescribably satisfying. He sat in the bar and savored a single-malt scotch while he went through his wallet. To his amazement, the departure date on his airline ticket was the next day. He had not missed his flight. And yet he had been so sure. For the first time, George felt a nagging doubt of his own mental powers.

At least, his ordeal was over. He'd fly back home and forget the horrible experience had ever happened.

George was mistaken. By the time he had flown back to the Twin Cities, a video of his adventures had gone viral on social media. There he was scuffling in front of the Homeless Center, sleeping under the bridge, and most humiliating of all, being arrested for stealing a sandwich. The voice-over was taken from his recent campaign sound bites. "Anyone with any intelligence can pull himself up by his bootstraps." "I have no sympathy for small time criminals and pickpockets. They should be locked up." "Only the weak beg for welfare." "No more funding for soup kitchens and homeless shelters. It only encourages dependency."

"Wow," Emily said. "What a tale! How did you make it all happen, Sophie?"

"I won't go into detail, but I do have computer skills." Sophie smiled and looked down modestly at her hands.

"Hacking?"

"The skills I need to do my job."

No computers were safe from invasion, Emily realized.

"My regular job providing temp workers gives me access to many places. Several of my people were at the hotel. I worked there as well. Nobody notices me really. And they don't expect me to be terribly competent. Delmar and I really hit it off."

"What about the video? How did you get that?"

"I use an excellent photographer with a long-lens camera, who knows how to keep a low profile. He's been useful on many of my projects."

"And I suppose you were Ethel?"

"Poor Ethel. The phone system was too much for her."

"Isn't she marvelous?" Vanessa gushed. "You can see why I'm so grateful. The hateful Mogg's political hopes were dashed. Not so much because of his heartless opinions and policies, but because he looked like a ridiculous loser. Exactly the kind of person he scorns."

"Would your father have been gratified?" Emily asked, recalling that gentle, self-effacing man.

A cloud passed over Vanessa's strong features. "Perhaps not. He was not as vindictive as I was on his behalf."

Chapter 5

The next morning Emily looked out on a lovely spring day. The snow had melted, the street was clear, and the sun shone. She had just stepped out of the shower when her phone rang. Emily rushed to answer it before it could wake Jack.

Vanessa's voice rang out. "Emily, I'm so glad I caught you. You're up and about, I trust?"

"Oh yes, sort of, but we still have to tuck into our English breakfast. What's up?"

"I'm worried. Sophie is no longer as confident as she was yesterday. Something has upset her terribly. She wants to see you, Emily. Can you meet her at Broadway Tower?"

"Any mystery reader will tell you that agreeing to meet a suspected killer in a remote location is going to end badly."

"Oh, Emily. You must know Sophie wouldn't harm a fly."

"Actually, I don't know that."

"Well, take my word for it. She wants you to meet her this morning. Somewhere quiet where she won't run into the constabulary."

Emily reluctantly agreed, her curiosity winning out as always. "But I'm not going alone. Jack is coming with me. As soon as he wakes up."

Later that morning after feasting on smoked salmon and eggs, Emily and Jack piled into the Land Rover.

"I'm looking forward to sightseeing now that the weather has improved," Jack said.

"Yes, it will be fun." Emily paused for a moment and then said with bright enthusiasm, "And now there'll be an added bonus."

"Oh?" Jack sounded wary.

"You'll meet Sophie, Vanessa's dear friend."

"The suspected murderess?"

"That's the one."

"In general, I like to avoid aiding and abetting criminals on the lam."

"Me too. Absolutely. Sophie's going to turn herself in, but first she has to talk to me. Up to now, she hasn't said much because of client confidentiality. But something has changed."

"A wise woman would confide in her lawyer at this point."

"Of course, she'll do that too. I mean, I assume so. But Vanessa insists that I pitch in and do what I can."

"What hold does Vanessa have over you that you leap at her command?"

"We were best friends at St. Agnes School from kindergarten through eighth grade."

"And that explains it? Time cannot wither her—"

"*Age* cannot wither her," Emily corrected. "But, as you know, Vanessa's very youthful, my exact age, twenty-nine, so no wonder she's not withered." She realized she was babbling.

"You have a lot of best friends. Where is this secret rendezvous to take place?"

"Broadway Tower. This actually works out perfectly because it's on the list of tourist attractions I meant to visit today. It's a great place to start a walk along the Cotswold Trail. Nobody will notice us there."

Emily tried to keep her tone breezy and the mood light. She did not mention that she was hesitant to meet

Sophie alone. She had been very impressed by the woman's powers to wreak havoc. Sophie seemed to take great delight in it. Emily didn't want to get too deeply involved on the side of a woman who sought revenge, not justice.

After Jack parked the car, Emily took his hand and they trudged up the hill. The day was mild and the grass was a brilliant shade of green on hills that seemed to roll on forever. But it was still chilly. Emily pulled her scarf up over her face as she leaned into the wind.

At the top of the hill providing a breathtaking view of the surrounding hills and valleys, stood a single tower with four tall turrets.

"Where's the rest of it?" Jack asked, staring up at the tower. "It looks as if they forgot to add on the main part of the castle. Did they run out of money?"

"No, this is it." Emily had done her research and was able to explain. "This is a folly, something that's absolutely pointless and useless. It was built by the famous landscape designer Capability Brown in the 18th Century for the Earl of Coventry, who lived way over there." Emily pointed across the hills. "The earl wanted to see a tower from his home. He thought it would add visual interest to an otherwise boring vista of endless hills and valleys."

"An odd idea."

"Eventually, the tower did come in handy. It was used to track enemy planes over England during both World Wars. And it inspired William Morris to begin a campaign to preserve historic monuments. As a matter of fact, I'm going to jot down a few notes." Emily whipped out her little red notebook.

Traveler's Tip: *You may wish to start your hike through the Cotswolds by visiting Broadway Tower, the Cotswolds' highest peak. From this height, you*

*can gaze out at medieval travel routes and hills and
valleys dotted with sheep. You may even see red
deer. Inside the tower you'll find three floors of
displays illustrating its history.*

At the foot of the tower, Emily saw an old woman,
her white hair straggling from under a wool scarf,
limping toward them on the dirt path worn smooth by
visitors circling the tower. She wore stout wellies and
leaned on a stick. Emily recognized the spaniel walking
at her heels. She waited for the "old woman" to come
nearer.

"Can you help me?" she quavered. "I've lost my
way."

Then the woman noticed Jack and did a double take.
She waited until a family of tourists had passed them
and gone into the tower. "Emily, I thought you were
coming alone," she whispered, dropping all pretense
that she was a stranger. Nobody was in hearing distance
now. "Vanessa told me you're good at resolving
misunderstandings that can occur when a crime has
been committed. It's hard enough for me to confide in
even one person. I don't know…" Sophie glanced down
the hill as if ready to bolt.

"This is Jack Flynn," Emily said quickly. "Think of
Tommy and Tuppence, or Nick and Nora. We work
together."

Jack looked at her in surprise. "I've been upgraded
from Watson?"

Emily nudged him and shot a shushing look.

"Well, all right," Sophie said. "Let's start walking. I
can explain what's happened as we go."

Emily and Jack followed Sophie down the hill, and
they turned onto a path into the countryside.

"For reasons I shall soon explain, I am no longer bound by client confidentiality. Now I can tell you how I came to be involved in Edward Westley's death.

"A few weeks ago, a middle-aged woman, conservatively dressed and dignified in manner, came to my temp office in London and told me she was a friend of Vanessa. Of course, I gave her my immediate attention. I think the world of Vanessa.

"This woman, who wore her dark hair in a bun at the back of her neck, said she was Beryl Westley, the wife of the M.P., Edward Westley. 'My husband and his family love to fool one another with elaborate practical jokes,' she told me. 'My husband is the champion.' Her bitter tone suggested this was on a par with being a convicted felon.

"'You don't enjoy these pranks as much as your husband does?' I asked her.

"'Nobody who wasn't raised in this peculiar tradition could derive as much pleasure from it as Edward does.' Suddenly, she leaned toward me and gripped my wrist. 'I need your help.'

"Her intensity made me uncomfortable. She had large expressive brown eyes that held me in their grip. 'I don't play practical jokes,' I told her. 'My services are more serious. I provide relief for people who are tormented by wrongs they have suffered and yearn for revenge. Unfortunately, your situation does not fall into that category, Mrs. Westley.'

"'I can see I have to be more forthcoming,' the woman said, twisting her handkerchief and raising anguished eyes to me. 'These pranks sometimes verge on the malicious. I never know when they will occur. I am becoming more and more anxious and tormented. I long to get even, to make my husband realize how much he has hurt me. I want him to suffer from the very sort of prank that would delight him if I were the victim.'

"Now I was becoming intrigued," Sophie said. 'Can you give me an example of the sort of thing he does?' I asked her.

"'Of course. There are so many to choose from. This was perhaps the worst.

"This is the tale the woman told me."

Beryl Westley's Story

One evening, Edward said he was going out, he had to work late. After he left the house and I thought I was alone on that stormy October night, I began to hear strange noises, clanking chains and groans, then muffled screams. My phone rang; I rushed to answer it, hoping to hear a sane, normal voice. All I heard was heavy breathing. I turned off my phone, made sure all the doors and windows were locked and went upstairs. As I reached the top of the stairs, the lights went out and I was plunged into total darkness. I heard a heavy clomping, like boots coming up the stairs.

I screamed.

Then the lights came on and I saw Edward standing halfway up the stairs, laughing. "I got you!" he cried. He rushed up and tried to hug me, but I pulled back, trembling. My heart was pounding.

"You are so gullible, my dear. I love it."

"It's not funny. I was terrified."

He couldn't stop laughing. "It's bloody hilarious. You have no sense of humor. Anita would be in stitches if my brother played this trick on her."

"I'm not Anita. It's not a trick. It's sadistic."

"Come, now, you're exaggerating. No harm done, right?"

Oddly enough, Edward thought terror would act as an aphrodisiac. He was sadly mistaken. That was the first night I slept in another bedroom.

Edward still didn't take me seriously. The next day, he shared his video with his family so they could join in the merriment.

"'So, you see why I need your help,' Beryl said after she finished her story.' I was intrigued by the possibility of punishing the insensitive brute she had married," Sophie said. "I asked this woman if she wanted to beat her husband at his own game. She told me she was anxious to do so. We had a brief conversation that gave me some ideas. She told me that Edward found snakes creepy. He had no fear of them, in fact, he kept a couple as pets when he was a boy and liked to scare girls with them. It wasn't a phobia, but a strong dislike amounting to revulsion. She also assured me he had no allergies or heart trouble. She wanted him to understand what it was like to be the victim for a change but, in the end, she expected him to be amused and chastened. She told me that she and Edward would be staying at The Black Swan in Chipping Campden, but in separate rooms, an arrangement that offered an opportunity.

"The anonymous letter claimed that Westley was terrified of snakes," Emily said. "How believable is this woman?"

"Not very, as you shall soon hear. But, at the time, I didn't doubt her and so I devised my plan accordingly. I told her what I meant to do. She approved.

"That night I let loose several Orange Ghost Ball Pythons in Edward's room and turned off the heat. I knew they would be drawn to his warm bed with its electrically heated mattress. Snakes have no way to regulate their body temperature and have to seek warmth. I had also arranged a bell pull beside the bed to remind him of the Holmes story, "The Speckled Band," to plant the idea that someone had trained the snakes to slither down the rope with the intention of striking him. These pythons are not poisonous, but they're more than a foot long and look extremely sinister. They were meant to give Edward at least a few minutes of anxiety. But certainly not to do him any serious, lasting harm."

"And yet he died," Jack said. "Why?"

"I don't know. The first news reports suggested he died of snakebite. I knew that was impossible so, I wasn't unduly concerned."

"Could you have unwittingly bought a poisonous snake?" Emily asked.

"No, I checked the markings very carefully. Then the next news report suggested Westley may have died of a heart attack. The coroner's report has not been released so I don't know if that's true, but it is certainly more troubling. Perhaps this woman didn't know about her husband's heart condition, I thought.

"I wanted to get her permission before I went to the police but the phone number she gave me had been disconnected.

"Since she had told me she was a friend of Vanessa, I thought I could ask her a few questions without violating my oath of secrecy. I suggested to Vanessa that this might have been a prank to get even with a man who, along with his family, loved practical jokes.

"Vanessa hooted. 'Edward Westley was a very serious man, grim, some would call him. He hardly ever cracked a smile. His entire family had always been reserved and would have been disgusted by pranks and hijinks. Now they're all dead anyway. He's the last of his line.'

"I didn't know what to think. Then this morning, I saw this photo of Beryl Westley in the newspaper."

Sophie rummaged in her carpetbag and pulled out a crumpled newspaper folded to reveal the frontpage story. "This is *not* the woman who hired me." She tapped her finger on a headshot of a woman with short brown hair, wearing pearls and a fascinator.

"You're sure? The photo's a little grainy. Perhaps she was dressed differently?"

"There's no resemblance. She's an imposter, someone pretending to be Beryl."

"How horrible," Emily said. "This false Beryl must have made up the story about the pranks. Maybe she knew that Westley really was afraid of snakes, so afraid that she could frighten him to death

"Looks like you were the victim of a scam," Jack said.

"Yes, I'm embarrassed to admit that I fell for this imposter's hoax. I had no reason not to believe her. Westley devotes his website to politics and policy. He has no personal information or photos of his family online. This woman's story was so compelling that I was eager to give the insensitive joker a taste of his own medicine."

Emily read the newspaper account aloud while Jack leaned over her shoulder, "Beryl Westley, wife of M.P. Edward Westley, told police she was appalled and heartbroken by his sudden death. Without his knowledge, she had booked a separate room in The Black Swan Inn, planning to surprise her husband in the morning. Instead she found a macabre scene, her husband lying dead in a bed filled with snakes. She has been under a doctor's care since the incident."

"I need your help, Emily," Sophie said. She didn't include Jack in her plea.

"I can't imagine what I can do."

"You can help me find out who this woman really is. The police will pull me in for questioning very soon, and I doubt they will believe my story. There is, however, a surveillance video of her entering my office. A video cam records everyone who comes in the front door. A sensible precaution, I think. With your permission, I'm going to ask my assistant Cyril to transfer a clip of the video into a format that you and the police can view, download it onto a flash drive, and mail it to you. You can give it to the police."

"What? Why me?"

"If I go to into my office, I'd be arrested before I could get it."

Emily sighed. "I don't know how helpful this will be. Is there audio? There usually isn't any sound on surveillance videos."

"Unfortunately, no. It's just a grainy black-and-white video. It doesn't prove anything, but it will help identify the imposter."

"Did you record the interview?"

"No, that would have been an invasion of privacy. Will you help me, Emily? You just have to bring the flash drive to the police station."

Jack interrupted. "Why a flash drive? Wouldn't it be easier for your employee to email it to you and to the police?"

Sophie stared at him as if her reluctance to include a strange man in their meeting was now fully justified. "The clip is much too large to email. Of course, I asked Cyril to mail a flash drive to me too but, I probably won't get it in time. I'll have to turn myself in today or risk being arrested. The police are closing in."

"Surely you could tell the police what happened and ask them to retrieve the video," Jack pressed her.

"What if they don't believe my story?" Sophie turned to Emily. "As soon as you get the video, take a good hard look at the woman who posed as Beryl. If Vanessa is right about your skills, you may be able to track her down. This video won't prove my innocence, but it will help you find out who she is."

"I think Vanessa has exaggerated."

"I have great confidence in her judgment. So much so that, anticipating your willingness to help, I've already asked Cyril to mail the flash drive to you at your hotel." Sophie said it as if she had just conferred a great honor on Emily.

Emily sighed. "I'll see what I can do."

Emily and Jack left Sophie trudging along the country lane, and headed back to the car park. As Emily slid into the Land Rover, she said, "Let's go on to Dover's Hill. It's quite close. Just about a five-minute' drive. I need to make some more notes for my article."

Jack agreed and, activating the Sat Nav, he turned onto Buckle Street and headed for their next destination. "You'd think Sophie would have checked a prospective client's identity more carefully," he said.

"True. I think Sophie was so intrigued by the possibility of fooling a fooler that she got carried away. I hope the police will believe her story and start looking for the woman who impersonated Beryl. She's the obvious suspect. She put Sophie up to putting snakes in Westley's bed, probably knowing he was terrified of them. Maybe Westley panicked and had a heart attack, as she intended. Or maybe False Beryl intervened in some other way to cause his death. I don't know why Sophie isn't more hopeful that the police will let her go and start looking for False Beryl."

"Possibly because after Sophie admits that she put the snakes in Westley's bed, the police might not trust her and might not even care who directed her to do it. And if they start to investigate Sophie, they may uncover her other shady practices as well."

"I suppose that's true. If they keep Sophie in jail, we might be the ones who are in the best position to figure out who the imposter is and why she wanted Westley dead."

Jack raised an eyebrow. "And yet, that is not our job."

Jack turned onto The Narrows then veered to the right into the parking lot. He and Emily climbed Dover's Hill and walked to the end of a plateau where there was a sheer drop-off. They stood, gazing down at the Vale of Evesham, a meadow far below where sheep wandered. In the distance Emily saw rolling hills fading to misty green and heard the faint baaing of sheep.

"It looks like the place where the sheep are driven off the cliff by the idiot dog in *Far from the Madding Crowd*," Emily said. "I always found that scene hard to picture but seeing this sudden, steep drop-off at the end of a large, flat plain, I can imagine the foolish sheep running straight ahead not noticing the field ended."

"You really are in English-major heaven, aren't you?" Jack grinned at her.

"Yup." Emily shared her research knowledge. "There's been a festival on Dover's Hill since medieval times. Head bashing with a stick was popular at first but because of the number of fatal injuries it was ended."

"No wonder."

"Another favorite is the shin kicking contest in which two guys kick each other on the shins trying to force their opponent to the ground. That still goes on."

"And I always thought Monty Python was so outrageous," Jack said. "Fish slapping would fit right in."

"A current favorite is the Cheese Rolling Race in which a wheel of Double Gloucester is rolled from the top of this hill and contestants run downhill to see who can catch the cheese first. In fact, nobody ever catches the cheese, which can roll as fast as seventy miles an hour, so the first runner to the bottom of the hill wins the cheese. Dozens are injured each year in this bizarre feat of strength. Perhaps we should have come in June. I would love to see the Cheese Rolling. It's part of the Cotswold Olympics."

"I wouldn't risk it. You'd probably plop down and start rolling yourself. You seem drawn to dangerous activities."

Noticing his serious expression, Emily guessed what he was thinking. "So, you're not sure it's a good idea to get involved with Sophie."

"I'm sure it's a *bad* idea."

"But it means so much to Vanessa."

Jack took her hand. "Clearly, Vanessa is very important to you. Why? You haven't seen her in years."

Emily sighed. "When we were kids, I spent a lot of time at her home. My mom and dad weren't getting along. I wanted to escape the shouting. Both Mom and Dad told me their version of every quarrel and I squirmed in embarrassment. I didn't want to take sides. I loved them both so I found reasons to be away. Vanessa's home was a perfect escape."

"Her mother adored anything British. Although she'd never been to England, she created a little bit of Britain in their home. They had tea every day. When the grandfather clock bonged three times, she served homemade shortbread and tea, brewed in a pot instead of from tea bags. She sewed dresses for Vivian made from Liberty print fabrics that she ordered from London. Of course, she kept us well informed about the royals' activities. British magazines and newspapers were stacked on the coffee table. A photo of Queen Elizabeth hung over the mantel. Vanessa and I loved the same books, *The Scarlet Pimpernel* and the stories of Sherlock Holmes. We played chess by the fireplace as we sipped our tea. It was lovely, very calm and civilized. I was always welcome to stay overnight.

"Vanessa was a loyal friend to me. When I was in fifth grade, my classmates thought I'd stolen Joanie Sullivan's new watch. There was a sneaky, whispering campaign and I saw friends looking at me sideways, not saying anything. I found out what was going on from Vanessa. She never doubted I was innocent. She didn't need proof or reasons why I didn't do it or even a firm denial. 'That's just not the sort of thing you'd do, Emily,' she said. Her words warmed my heart. She insisted we sneak back in school after hours and search the desks. I said there was no point. Who would be stupid enough to keep it there? Then we looked at each other. Annie O'Donnell. A girl who was so dim that when Sister asked her to name the seven acts of mercy, she misheard her classmates whispering the answer and said, 'Bury the sick and visit the dead?' So, she was our chief suspect. We found the watch in Annie's desk, stuffed way in back. Annie was the one who had started the rumors about me. The next day, Vanessa asked Sister to search all our desks. Annie was exposed as the thief. Then all my friends told me they had never believed I was guilty. But it was Vanessa's loyalty that made the difference. So, I understand the way she's sticking by Sophie, a woman who helped her when she needed help. She's a true friend."

"Vanessa was right about *you*. But is she right about Sophie?"

"I don't know, but I do know I have to help Vanessa. I trust her judgment."

Jack put his arm around Emily. "You're a loyal friend. Just remember, we don't know much about Sophie."

"True. Vanessa *thinks* she knows her well. But does she? Vanessa's loyalty could end up getting her involved in a crime."

"Or more likely getting *you* involved. Vanessa's not really taking the lead. Remember how she left you on your own with Sophie in the Churchill Arms."

"Yes. I suspected she didn't want to be there if Sophie was arrested."

"Now Sophie wants you to track down False Beryl, who may be a ruthless killer. I don't notice Vanessa joining in the search."

"She's just cautious because she's trying to protect her husband but she thinks the world of Sophie and believes she provides a valuable service."

"It worries me that Sophie seeks revenge, without giving any thought to justice," Jack said.

Emily could only agree.

"When I was doing my medical school rotation in the ER, I saw the results of revenge. Young kids, gang members, who were caught up in a cycle of revenge would be brought in bleeding, sometimes dying. There'd be one shooting, then the next night another in retaliation. Nothing was solved. Boys were dead. Sometimes innocent little kids were caught in the crossfire. In some neighborhoods, even if they were home watching TV, doing their homework, they weren't safe from gang violence."

Emily squeezed his arm. "That's horrible, but Sophie has nothing to do with that kind of violent revenge."

"Or so she says."

Chapter 6

Later that afternoon, after returning to The Noel Arms, Emily stopped at the front desk to ask if she had any mail, hoping the flash drive would have arrived.

"Nothing in the post today, madam."

Emily's shoulders slumped. "Well, then, I have no excuse not to work on my article, do I?" she asked Jack. Emily dearly loved her job as a travel writer, but, at the moment, she was distracted by Sophie's dilemma.

"None whatever."

"Let's walk through town and I'll take some photos."

"Good plan. We should end up at Eight Bells just in time for dinner," Jack said.

Emily led the way across the street to the Market Hall and took photos while she shared the fruits of her research with Jack. "When this hall was built in 1627, it was *the* place to shop and gossip." Walking on the rough cobbled floor and looking up at the arched roof and wood pillars, Emily could imagine the hall as it had once been, crammed with eager people buying and selling eggs, butter, cheese and bread. "It was built by Sir Baptist Hicks, the lord of the manor. You can see his coat of arms up there. He was a favorite of King James and he supplied his court with silks and finery."

"Amazing the hall's still standing," Jack said. "I would have expected it to be bulldozed and replaced by a quickie mart."

"Thank goodness that didn't happen."

Emily and Jack headed down High Street, which was wide enough for sheep to be herded to market. When they reached the Red Lion Inn, they turned onto Sheep Street where they found the Silk Mill, an Arts and Crafts shop, which sold hand-painted silk scarves and silver jewelry, as well as unusual and beautiful bow ties, all made by guild members. Emily couldn't resist buying scarves for her mother and sister. "The guild was started at the turn of the century when London artisans, who were rebelling against the Industrial Revolution, came here to sell handmade crafts," Emily informed Jack as she scooped up her purchases.

When they left the shop, the brief respite of temperate weather was over, and a cold wind was blowing in their faces. They had come to the end of the village. Before them was the Cotswold Trail, which wound through the countryside from one village to another. Emily and Jack started down the lane, bordered by fields of yellow rapeseed and pale blue linseed. Occasionally, they came upon a large house built of honey-colored Cotswold limestone with a thatched or slate roof. Emily took a few pictures, but her heart was not in it. She was wondering how on earth she could find Beryl's imposter.

Noticing her silence, Jack put his arm around her and pulled her close. "You don't have to get involved, Emily. I know you're worrying about Sophie, but it's not really your problem." He kissed the top of her head.

"Even if the photo is clear, which surveillance photos seldom are, how could I possibly find the woman?"

"You couldn't."

"Let's not be so quick to give up." Emily switched gears. "Who would have a motive to kill Edward Westley? That's what we have to find out."

"A formidable task. Sophie's the one to do it."

"Right, but if she's in jail, then what?"

"The police," Jack said.

Emily didn't answer. It was getting close to dinnertime, so they turned back to town. Emily stopped to point out the Grevel House. "This stone house, built by a prosperous wool merchant in 1367, was the first one in town. Its rain spouts were designed to look like gargoyles in order to frighten away evil spirits."

"Scary faces for sure," Jack said, looking at the ferocious stone imps, spewing water from their mouths.

Emily and Jack walked to the end of High Street and through a tree-lined lane to St. James Church, as magnificent as a cathedral. Inside, an organ was playing and a group of elderly people were gathering up their belongings and beginning to leave. Emily heard murmurs and rustlings as they walked past, smiling and nodding to her.

"An excellent practice session, Vicar,"

"Oh yes, indeed. Very good."

At the front of the church, Emily paused beside a canopied tomb where marble images of a be-ruffed Sir Baptist Hicks and his wife lay, sleeping for all time. "Here's the fellow who built the Market Hall," she said. "Sheep were very, very good to him."

"Evidently. He looks quite satisfied."

"He was a generous benefactor. He endowed almshouses for six poor men and six poor women and made sure they each had a small sum of money, a gown, a ton of coal and a new felt hat every year." Emily had done her research. "It reminds me of Trollope's *The Warden*.

As they left the church, Emily noticed a small tombstone that read, "Thank you Lord for Simon, a dearly loved cat who greeted everyone who entered this church. RIP 1980."

"What nice parishioners," Emily said. "It was kind of them to remember their cat."

After a delicious dinner of fish and chips at Eight Bells, a cozy pub of brick and timber with a fire roaring in the hearth, Jack and Emily headed back to The Noel Arms.

"A package for you, madam," the clerk said as he handed her their room key and a small padded envelope.

Emily couldn't wait to get back to the room. She put her laptop on the desk, woke it up and inserted the flash drive that she found inside the envelope. On the screen she saw a black and white image of a tall woman in a jacket and skirt walking briskly through a door. The woman glanced around, then stuck out her hand to Sophie, who entered the picture from the right. The screen went blank. That was it.

"The image of her face is clear but since there's no audio it certainly doesn't prove she impersonated Beryl Westley," Jack said.

"No, but it's a lead. If I can find out more about the victim, I might have some idea who would want him dead. This photo could narrow down the suspects. I'll copy a screen shot onto my phone."

"Remember, we don't know if Westley was murdered. He could have died of a heart attack."

"The imposter must have had some reason for hiring Sophie to play a trick that turned deadly. She may have known he was terrified of snakes. After all, the anonymous letter said that was common knowledge. I'm going to talk to Vanessa. She may know something."

Vanessa answered on the first ring. "I was just going to call you. Disaster, my dear. Sophie has been arrested! It was all over the evening news."

"I'm so sorry, but not surprised. She told us she thought the police were closing in when we met her this morning."

"Oh, good. What a relief. I didn't know if she had a chance to talk with you before she was apprehended."

"Oh yes. She told me that the woman who hired her was not Beryl Westley. She was an imposter. Now she doesn't feel bound to confidentiality. She was tricked."

"Yes, she told me that too. Before they nabbed her."

"Sophie had asked one of her employees to mail me a flash drive with the photo of the false wife from her office surveillance camera. I've watched the video several times. I'll give it to the police, but, outside of that, I don't think I can help."

"You can figure out who she is."

"How? Who would play a prank on Westley that was possibly meant to kill him?"

"I can't imagine. But you might start by going to the village where he grew up and talking to people who knew him. Someone is bound to have ideas. I'm relying on you, Emily."

"You do realize I have a writing assignment," Emily said. "I can't devote all my time to investigating on behalf of a woman I hardly know. She's *your* friend."

"Oh, Emily, I'd do it myself, but Nigel wouldn't hear of it. He'd be furious. Political repercussions, you know. Besides, you have a proven track record, a knack for this sort of thing and I'm absolutely hopeless. Do forgive me for imposing on you, but…."

"No, no, it's okay, I'll do what I can."

"Excellent! I knew you would come through trumps. You always have."

When Emily turned off her phone, Jack said, "Trying to weasel out of this assignment got you nowhere with the steely-eyed Vanessa, I suppose?"

"Sadly, you are correct. But I must say I am curious."

"Of course, you are. It's the thrill of the chase. The hound hears the clarion call of the bugle and is off. The game is afoot."

"If I may choose, I would rather you compared me to Sherlock Holmes than to a slavering hound."

Jack laughed. "I'll keep that in mind."

The next morning, Emily and Jack drove through beautiful rolling hills dotted with sheep and headed toward the police station in Stow on the Wold, which served several Cotswold villages, to deliver the flash drive.

"What a charming town," Emily said as they drove through the narrow streets, looking for the police station. "It's another wool town like Chipping Campden." Emily had done her research and knew that Stow's heyday had been in the Middle Ages when Cotswold sheep provided top quality wool that was sold all over Europe and England.

Emily pulled out her little red notebook.

Travelers' Tip: "Wool merchants in the Cotswold villages like Chipping Campden and Stow on the Wold grew rich and built beautiful homes of golden stone in Medieval times. Then during the Industrial Revolution, cotton became popular and the wool industry collapsed. The region was pretty much ignored. Now these charming villages look much as they did in the middle ages."

Jack parked the car in front of a beautiful stone building with one tall pointed window like that of a church as well as gables and mullioned windows. "Very grand for a police station," Emily said as she walked up to the building.

Jack tried the door, but it didn't budge, "Why would the police station be locked in midday?"

Emily rapped the knocker twice. The door opened a crack. "You'll have to go to Cirencester," an irritated voice said. "We're not open to the public."

"Are you a police officer?" Emily asked.

"Yes."

"I need to talk to you."

"I conduct investigations out of this station, but as you see, it's not open to serve the public."

"I don't want to be served. I have valuable information in a murder case."

The door swung open. An officer whose drooping jowls gave him the look of a lugubrious hound dog, introduced himself as Sgt. Collin Norville and allowed them to step into the hallway. Looking mildly curious, he waited for them to speak.

"We have information that may clear Sophie Morton. She's a suspect in the murder of Edward Westley and has been pulled in for questioning," Emily said.

"You're friends of Miss Morton?"

"Acquaintances," Jack said.

Emily held out the flash drive. "By now Sophie Morton must have told the police that she was hired to put snakes in Edward Westley's bed. This flash drive has footage from her office surveillance video that shows the woman who impersonated Beryl Westley and hired Sophie Morton." Emily didn't exactly expect the officer to yell "Wow!" but she was hoping for a more enthusiastic response than his bland, "Is that so, ma'am?"

"It should help you find the person who is really responsible."

"Thank you, Ms. Swift." Officer Norville accepted the flash drive and glanced meaningfully toward the door.

"You probably have ways to figure out who this woman is, don't you?" Emily persisted.

"We have the investigation well in hand."

"You will look for her, won't you?"

"I realize you are sympathetic to Miss Morton, but please understand this is a police matter. You have done your duty by passing along evidence to me." Sgt. Norville opened the door and showed them out.

"Not a particularly effervescent guy," Jack observed as they headed to the car.

"Laconic describes him best," Emily agreed. "I'm afraid he isn't going to pursue our valuable lead."

"We don't know that. He just may not want to share his plans with us. He made it clear he doesn't welcome help from civilians."

When they returned to their hotel, Emily combed the Internet for information about Westley. There was little personal information on his website, but she did find out he had grown up in Stow on the Wold. The only photos on his website were of Westley speaking at political events.

Emily typed in "News in Stow on the Wold" and the web page of the *Cotswold Journal* opened. Checking the archives for articles about Westley, she found him mentioned in a feature that was published a few years ago when his former nanny, Rose Wilson, retired. The article noted that she had later served as nanny to several other families, who praised her in glowing terms. Westley was briefly mentioned in the nanny's own quote, "My most famous charge is now an MP. Imagine that! And he was just an ordinary little chap. I had no idea he would be famous someday. How kind of him to come here today."

"Listen to this, Jack." Emily read him the quote. "Westley's old nanny may know something."

"He hasn't needed a nanny for years," Jack said.

"No, but apparently he kept in touch with her. This could be a lead."

Emily called Rose Wilson, introduced herself as a reporter, and invited her to lunch the next day at Lucy's Tea Room in Stow on the Wold. She said she wanted to interview interesting people who lived in the Cotswolds for an article in an American newspaper.

The next day, the sky was bright blue and the sun shining so Emily found the drive to Stow beautiful despite the snowy fields and drooping daffodils. She drove past the police station and up to Lucy's Tea Room, a stone building with a bow window, round as a cake, trimmed in white. Inside, Emily spotted Mrs. Wilson, the only woman sitting alone at a table. She had a broad, pleasant face with short white hair curling round it. After Emily introduced herself, the woman beamed at Emily and held out her hand. "How lovely to meet you, my dear."

Her manner was so warm that Emily felt as if she had run into an elderly relative, whom she had somehow forgotten. "It was kind of you to agree to talk to me," Emily said. "Let's order and then I'll ask you a few questions if you don't mind."

Emily ordered Welsh rarebit on crumpets and a salad while Rose chose squash soup, a cheddar scone and chutney. Both asked for tea. Over a delicious meal, Emily explained to Rose why she had sought her out. "I understand you were a nanny to Edward Westley. I'm investigating—"

Rose Wilson broke in with enthusiasm. "Oh, you're looking into his mysterious death for your article. I'm so glad. It was quite a horrible way to die especially for Edward. He was absolutely terrified of snakes."

Aha! False Beryl *had* lied. The information in the letter was right. "Was that common knowledge?" Emily asked.

"I shouldn't think so."

That narrowed the number of people who could have written the anonymous letter mentioning his fears. Emily watched Rose spread chutney on her scone and take a huge bite. Chewing slowed down her reminiscences for a moment, but Emily could see it was not going to be hard to pump her for information. "Mrs. Wilson, I would love to know more about Edward Westley."

"Please call me Rose, my dear. Of course, I hadn't seen Edward for years until he came down for my farewell party, so kind of him, all the way from London, and he such a very busy man, an MP no less."

"How did he become so afraid of snakes?"

"Oh, that *is* a tale. When he was just a little fellow, a family that lived quite nearby was on intimate terms with the Westleys—the Benson family. They had two children, Cyril, who was two years older than Edward, and Clare who was just his age. Their nanny would walk the children over to play and stay to chat with me. Edward adored Clare but he never cared for Cyril, who, I must say, could be a bit of a bully. Clare and Edward would go off together to walk in the woods or draw or read books in a little gazebo down by the river. Cyril wanted Edward to play tennis or practice cricket with him even though Cyril was a much better player. Well, that was no surprise. Cyril was bigger, stronger, older. He taunted Edward every time the boy missed a shot. Not the best way to get him to play another match. Cyril felt left out, I think. He was very close to his sister and he resented how much she enjoyed being with Edward. He was odd man out.

"Anyway, Cyril found a way to get even. One day we had a terrific rainstorm. A real cow quaker. Cyril came over alone. I built a fire and made tea for the children. Cyril had brought a book with him and said he wanted to read aloud to Edward. 'What a good idea,' I told him. His book turned out to be, not a story, but an illustrated book about poisonous snakes. Well, my dear, it was dreadful. Cyril could have been an actor. He was that dramatic in his reading. When he described how victims of snakebite died, it made my flesh creep. I saw how frightened it was making Edward and thought to myself, Oh, we'll have nightmares tonight, my lad, no doubt about it. 'That will be quite enough, Master Cyril,' I said. 'The rain has stopped now so you two can put on your wellies and go for a walk.'"

"Later, Cyril came back alone and told his nanny he wanted to go home. 'Where's Edward?' I asked."

"He wanted to walk by himself. Don't know why."

"That's certainly odd. Go out again and see if you can find him."

"Can't do it. My mum said to be home at four and it's nearly that now. Isn't it, Nanny Baxter? We have to go home, don't we?"

Baxter agreed. I was that frustrated but Cyril wasn't my charge. I put on my raincoat and walked toward the woods where the children used to play. I hadn't gone far before I heard sobbing. I called out to Edward. "Teddy, love, where are you?"

His crying grew into a scream. I rushed forward. And then I stopped in horror. The rain had brought out snakes that were slithering all over the ground. Edward stood with his back against a tree, frightened out of his wits, his fist jammed into his mouth to stop him from screaming again.

"You poor lamb, don't be frightened, "I said, pretending not to be disgusted by the slimy, slippery creatures. "These snakes aren't poisonous. Not at all like the wicked serpents in the book. Just little garter snakes.

"I stamped my foot and yelled, and the snakes slid off the path. I took Edward by the hand and led him home.

"That night when his father found out what had happened, he was furious at Edward. He accused him of being weak and cowardly, not fit to represent a historic military family. Tears ran down the little lad's face. I really felt sorry for him. He was only six years old.

"I'm afraid Edward never got over his fear and horror of snakes. At least not while he was in my care. Then he went off to school and I went to another family so he may have outgrown it. Still. What a horrible way to die."

"It is. Poor soul," Emily pulled out her phone, open to the photo of the woman who impersonated Edward's wife and handed it to Rose. "Do you recognize this woman?"

Rose put on her glasses and peered at the screen. "She looks familiar, but I'm not sure. Why do you ask?"

"She might be involved in the snake incident."

Rose handed back the phone as quickly as if it were red hot. "No! I have no idea."

"Who knew how Edward felt about snakes?"

"I couldn't say. I didn't see much of Edward after he went to school."

"What became of Cyril?" Emily was beginning to suspect the little bully had struck again.

"He went to Blanchley Hall too. At the same time Edward did."

"Where is Cyril now?"

"Oh, didn't you know? Well, of course not, how could you? He's dead." Rose looked rattled. She was gathering her woolen cloak around her and putting her glasses into her purse. "I must dash, but good luck to you, my dear. I have an appointment soon. I hope I've been of some help."

Emily called Jack who suggested they meet at the Lygon Arms. "I ran into a fellow who said he could vouch for its beverages," Jack said. "He looked trustworthy."

So, back in Chipping Campden, Emily stepped out of the wind into a cozy pub warmed by a wood fire and looked around the room twice before she recognized Jack. He was wearing a flat cap and handsome, tweed sport coat.

"Dear Jack, you look like a local," Emily said, stroking the fine fabric, admiring the thin lines of blue in the gray tweed. "All you need is a spaniel and you'll fit right in."

"That's the idea. This afternoon, I stopped at the Country Master store across the street from our hotel. The woman who waited on me said this jacket is just what a gentleman needs to wear at the Cheltenham Races. She was eager to outfit me top-to-toe, but I resisted. It's a men's store, along the lines of Hymie's in St. Paul but even more posh."

"You're going to Cheltenham? Whatever for?"

"I can't spend all my time sleuthing. Brendan, my distant cousin, has come over from Dublin for the races, and he invited me to join him at the track tomorrow. You remember. I've told you about him."

"Right, you spent a summer with him when you were in college."

"Yup. He's part of the Flynn family that stuck it out in Ireland when my great, great granddad came over to

America. We connected with the family years ago after my mother tracked them down through Ancestry.com and wrote to them. The upshot was we went over to Ireland to visit the Flynns one summer and hit it off. We all look surprisingly alike. Then, after my first year in college, I spent a whole summer in Dublin and Brendan and I became best buds. We've kept in touch through Facebook and emails ever since. That's why I feel comfortable driving on the *wrong* side of the road, as you call it. I drove Brendan's car that summer, especially on occasions when he'd been overserved. They're lovely people. You'll have to meet them sometime."

"I'd like that."

"I hinted that I had a wife who is keenly interested in racehorses but apparently this is an outing for the lads. Probably just as well. You have a lot on your plate."

Emily did love horse racing and longed to go with him, but she knew Jack was right. Between her travel articles and her need to find the false wife she was a bit overextended.

"If it's wonderful, we can go together another time," Emily said.

The server set down tall flute glasses filled with fruit and red wine. "Delicious," Emily said after tasting it. "Your new-found friend gave good advice."

As they sipped their fragrant beverages, Emily told Jack the story about Edward, who at six years old was led into a snake-filled wood and abandoned there by a bully.

"The horrible experience traumatized him," Emily said. "Rose didn't know if he ever got over it. Her reminiscences ended when Edward was just a boy. I suspect Rose knows more but, for some reason, wasn't willing to tell me. At first she said the woman in the photo looked familiar and she seemed to be struggling to remember who she was, but when I said she might be involved in the incident concerning Westley, Rose said she had no idea."

"Do you believe her?"

"I think she suddenly remembered who it was and didn't want to implicate her."

"Or maybe she just didn't want to get involved and stopped trying to figure out who it was."

"That's possible. But I have another lead. In the article about Rose's retirement there was a glowing quote about her by Bridey Maguire, a woman who worked as a housekeeper for the Westley family. She stayed on long after Rose had moved on to a family with younger children. Now Bridey Maguire works in a chocolate shop in Bourton on the Water. I imagine I'll have to try a few truffles before she's willing to confide in me."

"No doubt."

Chapter 7

Early the next morning, Jack, wearing his new country gentleman tweeds, was waiting in the hotel lobby for his ride to the Cheltenham races. A horn tooted and a Jaguar with its top down stopped outside the hotel. Brendan stepped out of the car to greet Emily, pump her hand and tell her how gorgeous she was. Then he turned to his cousin. "You lucky devil, Jack. A blonde Yankee girl with big blue eyes." He apologized for being in a terrible hurry and hopped back in the car.

Emily kissed Jack goodbye, wished him luck, then watched the racecar speed out of town.

Emily headed back to the hotel's sitting room where plaid easy chairs were arranged around a fireplace and settled down to begin jotting notes for her article.

Presently, she looked up to see Sophie and her dog walking toward her. "Good morning," Sophie said, as she sat in the chair beside Emily. She wore her Cotswold tweeds. Her spaniel turned around three times and lay down at her feet.

"I thought you were in jail," Emily blurted out. Throughout the sitting room, heads turned. Emily realized this was the sort of question that should be whispered.

"The police couldn't hold me any longer unless they filed charges. There's no evidence that I planted the snakes, much less had any intent to harm Edward."

"But you did plant the snakes."

"That's the allegation in the anonymous letter."

"So now you deny it?"

Sophie frowned and looked around the room. An elderly couple sitting across the room looked extremely alert even though their eyes were focused on their newspapers.

Emily lowered her voice. "Who could have written that letter?"

"I have no idea. Someone who has a grudge against me but I know of no such person."

"Really? What about all the people you have punished for their misdeeds?"

"If anyone found out who was responsible, I imagine they might want to get even," she said slowly.

"Oh? Do you think?" Emily imagined a horde of enraged people standing in line to get at Sophie.

Sophie shrugged.

"We did bring the flash drive to the police, but the officer didn't seem interested. I don't know if that was a factor in letting you go." Emily waited for effusive thanks but instead Sophie said, "I've come to ask a favor." She lowered her soft voice even more. "Can we go to a more private place? Perhaps my car? I'd like you to go somewhere with me."

"Where?" Emily's voice sounded as wary as she felt.

Sophie leaned over and whispered. "Beryl Westley's house. I want to explain and apologize for what happened to her husband."

Emily realized that Sophie's previous statement about an "allegation" was strictly for the benefit of eavesdroppers.

"At first Mrs. Westley was reluctant to see me, but I reassured her. I told her that a woman who is assisting the police with their inquiries would be with me. Finally, she agreed to let me come to her home."

"Why do you want me to come with you?"

"Because Mrs. Westley may know why someone would want to harm her husband. And she may recognize the woman who impersonated her. If the police decide to charge me, I won't be able to follow up and you will."

After a short drive, Sophie pulled her Mini Cooper up before a stone house with a thatched roof and roses climbing into an arch above the door. The woman who answered the door was tall and slender with short brown hair framing her face. She wore pearls and a twin set. With her eyes narrowed and mouth clamped tightly shut, she stared at them without saying a word.

Emily recognized the real Mrs. Westley from her photo in the paper.

Sophie moved closer to her. "Mrs. Westley, I'm Sophie—"

"I know very well who you are."

"My solicitor advised me not to come but I had to see you and apologize. I thought I was acting on your behalf when I played what I believed to be a harmless prank on your husband. I'm so very sorry."

"Harmless! Really? I wanted to see what a woman looked like who could do such a heartless, evil thing. Now I've seen. You can go."

"Please, I do deeply apologize, Mrs. Westley. I want to find the person responsible."

"Look in the mirror."

"Someone set me up. Someone, pretending to be you, hired me. I have to find that woman," Sophie said. "Please believe me. I never met your husband, Mrs. Westley. I had no reason to harm him. I was tricked into doing what I did."

"A bizarre, dangerous thing to do. Even if you were hired, you killed my husband."

"The coroner's report hasn't been released. Maybe his death wasn't caused by the snakes."

"Preposterous. Of course, it was."

Beryl turned to Emily. "Who are you? What are you doing here?"

"This is Emily Swift," Sophie answered quickly. "She's helping the police with their inquiries."

"In what capacity?"

"Just asking a few questions," Emily said. "Perhaps you know something that can help us find the person who planned this. I read in the paper that you were at the same hotel as your husband that evening."

Beryl looked suspicious, but after a moment, she answered. "Yes. I was going to surprise my husband."

"You didn't go to his room that night," Emily said. "You stayed in a separate room. Why?"

"What an impertinent question. I always had the impression Americans were ill bred. Now I see I was right." Beryl glared at Emily. "But I don't want to leave you with the impression that my husband and I were estranged or on any but the best of terms so, I'll gratify your rude curiosity. As I told you, my visit was intended to be a surprise. Edward had been staying at our flat in London for a couple of weeks and had just come down to the Black Swan for the night."

"Why would he stay in a hotel when his home is so near?" Emily asked.

"If you must know, our house was undergoing repairs. Thatch is dreadfully difficult and expensive to keep up. We had a man over, and it was noisy and messy. Edward hated that sort of thing. He comes here to relax." She winced. "*Came* here, I should say.

"I arrived at the hotel rather late and didn't want to wake Edward, so I took another room. In the morning, when I rang him, there was no answer. Edward was always an early riser, so I went to his room and knocked. When he didn't respond, I opened the door."

"You had a key?"

"Of course. When I checked in, I asked for a key to my husband's room as well as my own. The staff recognized me so there was no problem. We dine there often."

Beryl was becoming more and more distraught. Her eyes filled with tears. "I'll never forget how Edward looked when I opened that door. Sprawled on the bed with his eyes wide open and staring. His face was white, almost blue and, my God, those snakes. It was horrible." She turned on Sophie. "All your doing!"

Sophie pulled out her phone with a screenshot of the imposter. "Do you recognize this woman?"

"No. Why should I?"

"She's the woman who impersonated you and told me that her husband loved to play slightly sadistic practical jokes," Sophie said. "She wanted to teach him a lesson."

"What nonsense. Edward never played a joke in his life. He was a very serious man."

"She said his whole family loved practical jokes."

"He was an only child. His parents have been dead for years."

"Do you have any idea why this woman would want to harm Edward?" Sophie asked.

"None. I told you. I don't know who she is."

Beryl turned on Emily. "What is your relationship with the accused?" She sounded like a prosecutor.

"I don't have a relationship with her. I'm a friend of a friend."

"What friend?"

"Vanessa Chillingworth."

"So, you're friends of the Chillingworths, are you?" Beryl made it sound like an accusation.

"Yes, I've known Vanessa since we were children."

"She's certainly made a vulgar circus of that lovely old estate, or so I've heard. I would feel sorry for Lord

Chillingworth if he wasn't such a total ass. He must be pleased now that Edward's out of his way."

"I didn't realize they knew each other," Emily said. She recalled Nigel claiming that he'd never met Edward.

"My husband was all too familiar with Nigel. Through politics you know."

Emily didn't know and would like to find out, but Beryl was holding the door open wider.

"I'm sorry we made you relive this horrible experience," Sophie said.

"Believe me, I relive it every day."

After Sophie dropped her back at the Noel Arms, Emily ate a quick lunch in the bar and set out again. She had decided not to forewarn Bridey Maguire, the Westleys' former housekeeper, that she wanted to talk to her. With no idea how to pump this total stranger for information, Emily hoped that inspiration would strike.

After driving the Land Rover past sheep grazing in misty green fields, Emily stopped in Bibury to take photos to illustrate her article. She parked near a row of cottages of golden Cotswold stone standing before a stream that meandered into the woods. She followed the narrow path along the mill stream, where she shot photos of a moor hen, a small gray bird like a duck with a bright red beak, then aimed at a gorgeous male pheasant. He flew off rather than pose.

Emily quickly scribbled in her little red notebook.

Travelers' Tip: Bibury is well worth a visit to see the Arlington Row of gabled stone cottages where weavers once made cloth for the Arlington Mill. Now the mill is a museum with furniture from the Cotswold Arts and Crafts movement. William Morris, a leading designer, called Bibury, "the most beautiful town in

England." Quite a compliment since the Cotswolds are full of lovely little towns.

After a brief stop in town at a shop filled with William Morris memorabilia, Emily bought a few tea towels with his beautiful, floral Arts and Crafts designs then drove on to Bourton on the Water. She was glad that the Cotswold villages were so close together that she could drive between them in less than a half an hour.

As Emily parked the Land Rover, the sky was darkening, and rain threatened. She took her chubby, a short umbrella, and crossed the stone bridge over the canal. Even under cloudy skies, Bourton on the Water, called the "Little Venice of the Cotswolds," looked charming. Emily walked quickly toward the chocolate shop.

Inside Chocolate Temptations, Emily was engulfed in a marvelous aroma. Minding the counter was a woman with a broad ruddy face and bags sagging under bright blue eyes, who she assumed was Rose Wilson.

The woman smiled at Emily and pushed back ginger hair that showed an inch of gray at the roots. "Welcome, dearie, feel free to look around."

As she admired the confections, Emily chatted with her in what she hoped was a friendly, engaging way. Emily took her time, choosing dark chocolates with fillings ranging from violet cream to salted caramel.

Finally, as she handed over British pounds, Emily leaned forward and looked into the woman's eyes. "Are you Mrs. Maguire, by any chance?"

The woman drew back. "I'm Bridget Maguire. Known as Bridey. Not Mrs. I never married. Never saw the need."

"I'm so pleased to meet you. I had lunch with Rose Wilson in Stow yesterday, such a lovely woman. I

understand you two worked together at one time."
Without actually lying, Emily intended that Bridey
would assume Rose had suggested that she contact her.

As she hoped, Rose's name affected a quick thaw
and she invited Emily to call her Bridey. "We had good
times together, me and Rose, and that's a fact. Of
course, we were young back then. The last time I saw
Rose was at her Farewell Garden Party. I wouldn't have
known her. She's fattened up a bit. But then, I suppose
she wouldn't have known me either. Got me wrinkles
now."

"Rose was very helpful to me. I'm trying to find out
how Edward Westley died."

"Oh, that was a tragedy! He was a fine lad. You
know, I was housekeeper to the family until he was a
grown man, so I knew him well. He didn't deserve to
come to such a terrible end."

"I'd love to talk to you about him. Miss Maguire,
can I offer you lunch or tea? Do you close the shop at
all?"

"Today, you can bet I'm closing the shop. It's the
Cheltenham Gold Cup, isn't it? I'll be over to
Kingsbridge Pub watching it on the telly. Along with
everyone else in town."

"My husband is at the track right now. I would love
to see that race. Can I treat you to tea?"

"I'd be too excited to eat a morsel, but I wouldn't
say no to a pint of cider. You see I'll have a bit of a
flutter on the Irish longshot Rebel Dancer. The big race
is at 3:30, but we could nab a table near the TV if we go
now. It'll be that crowded."

Bridey Maguire put a notice on the door advising
shoppers that Chocolate Temptations was closed for the
afternoon. Rain was pelting down, so she and Emily
opened their umbrellas and hurried across the stone

bridge to the Kingsbridge Inn. Emily tucked her box of chocolates well away from the rain to protect it.

The bar was festooned with Irish flags and banners. Bridey waved to the barman who called out, "I've saved you a table, Bridey, but it's a good thing you're here. I couldn't have held it much longer."

"Good man, Liam."

Settled at the table, Emily ordered a cider and invited Bridey to have one too. "On second thought, I'll have a pint of Guinness," Bridey said. "A race like this calls for stronger stuff." To break the ice, Emily asked Bridey about the race. As she expected, the woman was eager to talk as she sipped the creamy froth off the dark brown ale.

"All the top Irish horses come over for the Cheltenham Festival and half the young men in Ireland come to cheer them on. The biggest race is the one today—the Gold Cup. It's a little more than three miles of steeplechase jumps. The horses have to jump over twenty-two fences, bless their hearts. Oh, it will be thrilling. There are thirty-eight horses running, most of them Irish. I think I've picked the winner and luckily not many folks agree so I'll be in the money if he comes through."

"Bet him to win, did you?"

"Never, dearie. Across the board. A smart bet."

Emily knew her father would agree. She had spent many happy afternoons at Canterbury Downs learning to handicap and bet. Eager to ask questions before the start of the big race, Emily took out her phone with the photo of the impersonator and slid it across the table. "Do you know her?"

Bridey leaned forward and looked closely at the screen. "I certainly do. That's Clare Benson."

Emily was astounded but tried not to show it. She didn't want to stem Bridey's confidences.

"She was often at the Westley's house. Edward adored her. They were playmates when they were little and then in their teens...well you know how that goes." She raised one eyebrow and took a swig of Guinness.

"When I saw her at Rose's Garden Party, she looked quite glamorous. She's an actress now, you know. I've even seen her on the telly a few times. But she usually acts in a small rep company in Stratford—not the famous RSC. That's the Royal Shakespeare Company, you know. Clare told me she preferred the smaller stage and more intimate setting. Oh, really? It was all I could do not to laugh. You can bet your boots she'd snap up the chance to be at the RSC if they'd have her. Still, she's doing what she wants to do, and I always liked Clare. She was a sweet little girl. After the tragedy, of course, she wasn't the same, no one was."

Emily leaned forward. "What tragedy? Who wasn't the same?"

"Shhh. The horses are coming onto the track." Bridey took a gulp of ale and focused her full attention on the TV. The bar was packed now, and people were cheering.

Emily recalled that Rose had said Clare's brother Cyril was dead. At that point, she had become flustered and eager to end their conversation. After the race, Emily would press Bridey for more information.

Unlikely as it was that she would spot Jack at the track, Emily looked for him anyway. The enormous crowd made the Minnesota State Fair look like a ghost town. The steeplechase turned out to be totally unlike American racing or show jumping. Emily found it thrilling to watch the powerful horses jump solid fences that looked like natural hedges, then race flat out, maneuvering for position on the straightaways. Bridey was on her feet, screaming encouragement to Rebel Dancer from the moment the horses were away. She was hoarse by the time she sank back in her seat, gasping for breath, fanning herself with a napkin.

"He did it, God love him."

Her chestnut horse had come in a close second to a big bay.

After the race, Liam came over to the table and grinned at Bridey. "Good on you."

"Fork it over, love," Bridey said to him, holding out her hand. "You didn't believe he could do it, did you?"

"No, and he didn't."

"Well, he came close. Placing isn't bad."

Liam slipped some bills into Bridey's hand. "No, it's grand. And it was an Irish horse that won the Gold so I'm happy."

Bridey ordered another Guinness to celebrate. "My shout," she said to Emily.

Emily, who had to drive back to Chipping Campden, chose lemonade.

After Bridey settled down and stopped recalling high points of the race, Emily said, "You mentioned that Clare Benson was never the same after the tragedy. What happened?"

"Her brother Cyril was killed in an automobile accident when he was just eighteen. Clare was shattered."

"How horrible. Was she close to her brother?"

"Oh, when they were little, they were thick as thieves. But they quarreled a lot once they were in their teens. Cyril was jealous of the boys she dated. They wouldn't do unless they were chums of his or very rich. One time Cyril found Edward and Clare in the gazebo, knees up. He went into a rage, punched Edward and broke his nose. He told him never to come near the house again. He turned on Clare next, called her a little slut. Clare was furious. She said she would never forgive Cyril for humiliating her like that. She refused to ever speak to him again.

When he went back to Blanchley Hall, Clare didn't even say goodbye. Then after the accident, she was heartbroken. Poor girl."

Chapter 8

When Emily arrived back at the Noel Inn, she was disappointed to find that Jack hadn't returned from the races. Eager to tell someone her startling news, she called Vanessa and blurted out, "I've found out who the false wife is!"

"No! You're a marvel. Who?"

"Her name's Clare Benson. Apparently, she was a childhood friend of Edward's, but there was some sort of rift after her brother died. She's an actress who lives in Stratford. Luckily Jack and I will be going there the day after tomorrow. It's the next stop on my itinerary for the travel article. Do you know her?"

"The name doesn't ring a bell."

"I'd like to show you her photo."

"Come on over tomorrow. We'll be overrun with small children on a school trip to see the falconry show, ride the ponies and so forth, but Nigel can handle them."

Emily tried and failed to picture Nigel herding small children but didn't comment. After making arrangements with Vanessa for the next day, Emily put away her phone and looked out the window hoping to see Jack return. No such luck.

Still feeling too revved up from the day's adventure to settle down and read or write, Emily went down to the hotel pub where she found a trio playing traditional folk songs.

She was sitting at a table drinking a pint of lager, tapping her foot to the beat, when Jack came in looking disheveled and somewhat the worse for wear.

"I thought I'd find you here." Jack kissed her and sank down in a chair beside her.

"Too long a day at the fair?" Emily brushed a lock of black hair away from his eyes.

"You could say that. The races were fantastic, very exciting. Brendan and his friends are a fun-loving bunch. Also, very thirsty lads. Brendan had planned to run me home in his Jag but he felt he'd been overserved and wasn't ready for the road. Probably a wise decision. He's an impetuous driver even when he's cold sober."

"How did you get back?"

"The bus. It's pretty handy but it takes a while because it stops in all the little villages. Brendan's leaving tomorrow, flying back to Dublin on Ryanair or I'd suggest we get together. He's concerned about his sister Nora. He says, she's a "bit too bony," making a joke of it, the way he does but I could tell he was worried that she might be anorexic or at least heading in that direction. He wants to get back to her. His Uncle Valentine refuses to see a problem. 'She looks grand,' he says. 'You're just looking for trouble. Leave the lass alone.' It drives Brendan crazy."

"So, his Uncle Valentine's in denial."

"If you don't see it, you don't have to do anything about it."

"What about the parents?"

"They died when Brendan and Nora were young teens and Uncle Valentine took them in. Now Nora is at Trinity College. Brendan has a flat in Dublin and is working at an ad agency. Valentine's country house in Kilkenny is close enough to Dublin for them to visit him often."

"Poor Nora. I hope she'll be okay. I'll meet the family on another trip."

"Yes, I told him you wanted to get to know the Irish Flynns. Anyway, it was great to spend some time with Brendan. A thrilling race too."

"I know. You'll be surprised to learn that I saw the Cheltenham Gold Cup on TV and cheered enthusiastically for the horse that finished second."

"Did you really?"

Emily explained how she had interviewed Bridey, discovered that the false wife was an actor named Clare Benson, and helped cheer on Rebel Dancer.

Jack was suitably impressed.

The next morning, Emily and Jack met Vanessa at the door of Chillingworth Manor. Vanessa air kissed them both then led them through the house and out the French doors. "Come into the garden. Nigel is down at the birds-of-prey area already. The raptors are interesting to watch. Would you like to see them?"

After hearing assurances that there was nothing they would like better, Vanessa led the way along the pathway through the formal rose garden edged with purple sage and down to the raptor area.

Standing at the edge of a field was a group of children in school uniforms, boys in blue blazers, striped ties, shorts and knee socks, girls in plaid skirts, blazers and straw hats with ribbons.

"How adorable!" Emily said. "I love the uniforms." She had not loved her own uniform at St. Agnes, which had been hideous. These little girls looked as if they'd stepped off the page of a Madeline book.

One little girl was hopping on one foot. "Stand properly, Alice!" her teacher snapped.

"But I have a naughty leg," the child wailed.

The teacher grabbed her by the arm. "Teach it some manners."

Nigel quietly shook hands with Emily and Jack. "Welcome," he whispered. "I'm glad you've come. I'm quite proud of my birds." He looked up and pointed as a huge raptor flew low, barely clearing their heads, stirring a rush of wind.

The falconer, wearing a medieval tunic, held out his leather hawking glove and let the bird alight, and then gave it a chunk of meat. "Henry is a Harris Hawk," he told the children. "He's three years old. I've trained him to come to me by offering him food. It takes a good deal of patience. Have any of you children ever trained a dog? Or helped your mum or dad train one?"

A few hands went up.

"This is much harder. The hawk is a wild animal. But he does respond to food. Now I'll let him go." He lifted his arm, and the hawk soared above their heads, then high into the air circling slowly. "He's looking for prey. He'll swoop down if he sees a mouse or vole. His eyesight is incredibly keen. He can spot a very tiny animal from way up above the trees."

The falconer whistled, held out his arm again and the bird swooped down and alighted, gulping the chunk of food he fed him.

"That wraps up our program for today, boys and girls," the falconer said. "Your teacher will lead the way to the pony pavilion."

"You got here just in time," Nigel said. "Come meet our falconer."

The falconer briefly greeted them, then said to Nigel, "You'll be wanting to work with Henry before I put him away, I suppose."

"If you wouldn't mind."

"Here, put on the glove and take the lure. He'll like you all the better for having a bit of meat in your hand."

Nigel held out his glove and the hawk hopped over, settled with a ruffling of feathers and stretched out his neck to take the lure. Then he squawked and opened his wings, flapping rapidly. Nigel let him go. "It's thrilling really," Nigel said, looking up at the sky where the raptor was soaring. "I feel connected to my ancestors who lived here hundreds of years ago and hunted with hawks in this very field."

Emily realized that despite Beryl Westley's jibe, calling the manor a "circus," Vanessa had made it possible to preserve what Nigel loved best, the estate where his family had always lived.

"I took a course at Warwick Castle to learn how to hawk," Nigel said. "You can do that, you know." He nudged Jack. "Why don't you give it a go?"

Back home in Minneapolis hawks perched on the lampposts along on the freeway. Emily hoped Jack was not going to start luring them down with chunks of meat. She was relieved that he just chuckled at Nigel's suggestion.

After the hawk had been put in its crate, Nigel led the way back to the manor. Jack fell into step beside him. The men seemed deep in conversation so Emily felt she could talk to Vanessa without attracting Nigel's attention.

Emily took her phone with the photo from the security camera out of her purse and held it out to Vanessa. "This is Clare Benson, the actress who impersonated Mrs. Westley. Have you ever seen her?"

Nigel wheeled around. Apparently, he had superhuman hearing. "Of course, she hasn't. How would my wife know a British actress who goes around impersonating people?"

Vanessa shrugged. "Nigel's right. She doesn't look familiar and I don't recognize the name."

Nigel resumed his conversation with Jack and Emily began to chat, confiding in Vanessa about Jack's relationship with the Flynns, his friendship with Brendan and his concern for Nora. Vanessa listened and made sympathetic noises, as a good friend should. After the men had fallen a good way behind them, Emily lowered her voice. "I wanted to call Sophie and tell her about Clare, but I don't have her number."

"No, Sophie's very secretive. She won't give it out. But I can contact her."

Emily was a bit annoyed. "She doesn't have any trouble tracking me down when she needs me. Sophie dragged me along to see Mrs. Westley. She wanted to apologize."

"How did that go?"

"Mrs. Westley was not inclined to forgive. She was furious. But very British and self-possessed."

"That sounds like Beryl."

"Do you know her?"

"Not really. I've run into her at political gatherings."

Emily looked for Nigel and saw him up by the house, well out of hearing range. "Beryl Westley said something odd. She said Nigel would be glad that Edward was out of his way. What did she mean?"

"Oh, that's just nonsense. Nigel barely knew Westley. But he did think that for some reason Edward was preventing him from being assigned to committee memberships, plum party assignments, that sort of thing."

"That's strange."

"Very."

"He'd met him then?"

"Oh, yes."

"Did Westley have something against Nigel?"

"No. How could he? They were mere acquaintances. Maybe Edward did the same thing to other men, blocked their rise to power. He may have had strange quirks and prejudices that we know nothing about. Reasons why many men would be glad to see the last of him."

"How did Nigel feel about Edward's attitude toward him?"

"Mildly annoyed, I should think."

Later, back in her hotel room, Emily searched the web for Clare Benson and found her web page. Photos showed Clare playing the title role in *The Duchess of Malfi* at Another Stage in Stratford. Emily recalled from college that the play was a particularly gory Jacobean drama, exploring the grim themes of incest, jealousy and cruelty. Emily shivered. Under "Coming Next," she saw that Clare would play the role of Bel-Imperia in "The Spanish Tragedy," by Thomas Kyd, another bloodthirsty Jacobean revenge tragedy. It was now in rehearsal, scheduled to open in a week. There was no information about Clare's home address or ways to contact her. Emily would have to track her down at a rehearsal.

The chirping of her phone interrupted Emily's online browsing.

Sophie's voice was enthusiastic. "Good work. Vanessa was right about you. So, the wife's impersonator is Clare Benson. Vanessa told me to call you for details."

Emily was oddly pleased at her praise. "Yes. The Westley's former housekeeper recognized the woman in the photo right away. Now I know where I can find Clare and ask her some questions."

"Excellent. I want to go with you to confront this woman."

"Well then, come to Stratford tomorrow. We can accost her after the rehearsal of "The Spanish Tragedy."

"Bel-imperia, I suppose."

"Got it in one." Emily was surprised that Sophie was so familiar with the play. Then she recalled that Sophie had a background in theatre.

They made plans to meet at the theatre in late afternoon.

Shortly after Emily ended her phone call with Sophie, Jack burst into the room shaking his umbrella, sending droplets flying. "Horrible out there. It's cold and pouring rain."

"I'm going to soft pedal March weather in my article," Emily said. She brought Jack up to speed on her online discovery.

Jack peered over her shoulder at the photos of Clare Benson as the Duchess. "A powerful looking woman," he said.

"And yet Sophie described the false wife as a mild-mannered British matron."

"Perhaps it's the costume or the dagger that makes her look so forbidding."

"Well, she is an actor. One who seems to have bested Sophie at her own game. We can form our own opinion of Clare tomorrow."

"Do you think you'll be allowed into the rehearsal?"

"I'll think of a way. I'm a resourceful reporter, remember?"

"Be careful. This is a woman you suspect of orchestrating a murder."

"I won't be alone. There'll be you, me and Sophie. Clare will be outnumbered."

"What do you know about Clare? Besides her uncanny ability to impersonate."

"I know her brother died in an accident," Emily said. "I'll see what I can find out about it."

After a lengthy search of old archived articles on the web, Emily found a brief notice in the *Chipping Campden News*.

In a tragic accident, Cyril Benson, age 18, was struck by a motorcar in Chipping Campden Tuesday evening and died of his injuries. He was taken by ambulance to the North Cotswold hospital where he was pronounced dead on arrival. The Gloucestershire Constabulary is investigating the cause of the fatal mishap. He has not disclosed the name of the driver or whether alcohol was involved. Cyril Benson, who recently completed his studies at Blanchley Hall, had planned to attend Oxford in the fall. His bereaved father described him as an excellent student and keen sportsman.

"Poor kid," Jack said.

"Bridey told me that Clare was never the same after the accident. Do you suppose Edward was the driver? That would certainly give her a motive."

"Could be. Maybe Edward's name was withheld because he was a juvenile. That would make sense if he was two years younger than Cyril. A boy just learning to drive."

"Why would Clare want revenge after all this time?"

"Or ever? For an accident that happened when Edward was a boy."

Later that evening, Jack and Emily were enjoying a beer in the hotel bar when the television coverage shifted from a program on sheep shearing to the news of the day. When the photo of Edward Westley appeared in the corner of the screen, Emily jumped up and moved closer to hear the newsreader.

"Citing new evidence, the Gloucestershire Constabulary have issued an arrest warrant for Sophia

Morton, who was released yesterday after being questioned in connection with the death of Edward Westley, M.P. A police spokesman said he was not at liberty to reveal the nature of the new evidence."

Jack came over and stood beside Emily, his arm around her, looking at the screen.

Emily turned to him and whispered. "It looks as if Sophie's not going with us tomorrow."

On screen flashed a headshot of Sophie. "The police are attempting to locate Ms. Morton. Anyone with knowledge of her whereabouts is asked to call the Gloucestershire Constabulary." A phone number scrolled across the bottom of the screen.

"Uh oh, she's on the lam again," Jack said.

"I wonder why. What can the new evidence be?"

Jack shrugged.

The television coverage switched to another program on herding sheep this time.

The next day, after checking out of the Noel Arms and driving twelve miles through misty countryside, Emily and Jack pulled into Stratford upon Avon and stopped at the Adelphi House, one of several bed and breakfasts facing Ely Park. Their proprietor Sue greeted them warmly and asked if they wanted a cup of tea. Of course, the answer was "yes." She showed them into the front parlor where a table was set for them beside a bow window looking out on a park. Emily leaned over to inhale the fragrance of the lilies in a crystal vase on the lace tablecloth. Sue brought them a pot of tea, homemade gingerbread and frosted cupcakes. Her husband Simon sat down, armed with a map and sightseeing advice. "Such a lovely welcome," Emily murmured, sipping her tea. Jack agreed. Simon showed them on the map how to find Another Stage, "A short walk. You'll find it easily," he assured them.

Their room was on the first floor with French doors opening onto a patio where a table and chairs were set next to a small orange tree. On a warmer day, it would be lovely to sit there with Jack and enjoy a glass of wine. Emily and Jack hastily unpacked, then set out to find The Other Stage. Under cloudy skies, they crossed through a grove of sycamore trees in Ely Park where daffodils and crocus were scattered in the tall grass and continued into the town of Stratford upon Avon.

"It looks as if this town hasn't changed much since Shakespeare's time with all the half-timbered Tudor buildings," Jack said.

"It's beautiful, a mecca for English majors. I wanted to share it with you." Emily smiled at him. Jack squeezed her hand.

They walked across town to the River Avon and strolled along its banks until they came to a brick building labeled, "Another Stage." A sign tacked on the door read, "Closed." Underneath was a playbill announcing that performances would start in a week.

Emily pushed the door open and Jack followed her into a darkened corridor. Emily could hear raised, muffled voices. She slowly opened the door and looked inside to see an empty auditorium and a thrust stage where two players faced one another. Emily recognized the woman as Clare Benson from her publicity photos rather than from the security camera footage that showed her disguised as a nondescript matron.

A man sitting in the third row turned and looked back at them, then scrambled to his feet and bustled down the aisle toward them. "Oi! You can't come in here. We're not open. Surely you saw the sign. This is a rehearsal." His impatient words tumbled over one another. The man had a mop of two-toned black and gold hair and a Van Dyke beard that made him look part punk, part Elizabethan. He darted glances over his shoulder at the stage, apparently anxious not to miss anything.

"I am sorry," Emily said. "I know you're in rehearsal. I'm a reporter from the U.S. and I'll only be here a few days. Sadly, I'll miss your opening night. But I thought it would be fascinating to write about productions that are alternatives to the Royal Shakespeare Company, something a bit out of the ordinary."

"Oh, I see." The man's impatient manner dropped like a cloak. He bent toward her. "We are quite close to opening night. This is, in fact, the first dress rehearsal of one of the most important scenes, but it's not like seeing an actual production."

"I know. But I can get a pretty good idea from watching a rehearsal. I'm with the *Twin Cities Daily News*." Emily handed over her business card.

"I'm Trevor Norton, by the way. The director. This scene is near the end of the play."

"Perhaps I could just watch the rest of this rehearsal, then interview the actors. Do you mind?"

Trevor looked at Jack. "And you are…"

"This is my colleague, Jack. He's assisting me," Emily whispered. "We'll be very quiet."

Apparently, they were not quiet enough.

The actress on stage turned to face them and bellowed, "You there. What the bloody hell is going on?"

"The media, my dear. So sorry. Do go on."

"You've broken my concentration." Clare sounded as angry as if he'd broken her nose.

"Sorry, sorry. Let's take it from 'Tyrant, desist soliciting vain suits.'" Trevor picked up the script with a trembling hand."

Clare Benson, clad in a medieval gown of rich red and gold, wore her black hair gathered into a snood.

Her square jaw, dark eyes, and ivory skin emphasized her power and beauty. She took a deep breath, turned away, then whirled to face the audience once more, her dark eyes blazing.

"Tyrant desist soliciting vain suits. Relentless are mine ears to thy laments as thy butcher is pitiless and base, which seized on my Erasto, harmless knight." Clare took a dagger from the folds of her gown and lunged forward, her teeth bared. "But, were she able, thus would she revenge thy treacheries on thee, ignoble prince." She stabbed the actor, who was scrambling backwards, hands upraised to fend her off. He reeled and fell to the ground.

Then Clare lifted the dagger high above her head, pointed at her breast. "And on herself she would be thus revenged." She plunged the dagger into her bosom and crumpled to the ground.

"Brava!" Trevor called out, clapping. "That was lovely. I do wonder though if you might dial it back just a little."

Clare rose to her feet and glared at him. "Whatever do you mean?"

"We want the audience to feel pity for poor Bel-Imperia. You seem a bit Lady Macbethish."

"Nonsense, Trevor. Bel-Imperia is a strong woman who's forced to take over when the men are too mealy mouthed to wreak revenge on a killer. I thought we agreed on our approach."

"Just a thought, Clare. Do consider it. We can break now. These good people would like to interview you for an American newspaper."

"Ahh. Well, come up on stage then," Clare commanded. "I need to check on some of these props." She turned to the other actor who was already on his feet. "Are you okay? I didn't strike too hard, did I?"

The actor shook his head. "I think we're ready for opening night, Clare. I'll be on my way if you don't mind." He waved to Trevor and exited stage right.

Emily left Jack sitting beside Trevor, who was taking notes, and went up on stage where she found herself in the set of a medieval garden. She introduced herself to Clare and repeated her spiel about wanting to write about an alternative production. "Your role, a woman who is being callously disposed of by her brother and is forced to take the law into her own hands will appeal to today's audiences...and to my readers. Can we meet to talk about it? Can you join me and Jack for a glass of wine at the Garrick?"

"Not possible. I'm busy. Ask me any questions you have right now."

Emily had hoped to lead up gradually to Clare's role in planting the snakes. Now her plan was stymied.

"Well, out with it," Clare snapped. "I haven't got all day." She glanced at the clock in the back of the theater. "I can give you five minutes. Go."

Emily took a deep breath. Forced to drop the ruse of an article, she went straight to her real objective, hoping she could shock Clare into giving an honest answer. "Why did you hire Sophie Morton to plant snakes in Edward Westley's bed?"

Color drained from Clare's face. Her eyes glittered. "How in hell? Who are you? What are you really doing here?"

Emily dived into her purse and pulled out her phone with the screenshot from the security camera. She held it out to Clare. "I believe this shows you greeting Sophie Morton, just before you hired her."

Clare advanced on Emily, her dagger still in her hand, pointed forward. "Where did you get that?"

Instinctively, Emily backed up.

"Stop!" Jack yelled. "Emily, stop right there."

Emily turned and saw that one more step would have sent her plunging backward off the stage. Jack rushed down the aisle and hurried up the steps to the stage.

"Don't point that dagger at me." Emily pushed the blade away.

"For God's sake. It's just a prop."

Jack put his arm around Emily. "Watch where you're going, Ms. Benson. You could have forced Emily off the stage. She could have been seriously injured."

Trevor yelled, "What's going on?"

"Nothing, Trevor." Clare turned to Emily. "All right. Let's go to the Garrick. There's no reason for Trevor to get involved in this."

The Garrick, the oldest pub in a very old town, was half timbered, dark and cozy. In the back room, Jack ordered them each a glass of wine.

"Where did you get the photograph?" Clare came straight to the point.

"It was on the security camera in Sophie's office."

"I assume you're not a reporter but a private detective of some sort. You lied to me."

"No. I really am a reporter for the *Twin Cities Daily News* and I may even write about Another Stage but I am also helping Sophie Morton defend herself against charges that she deliberately tried to kill Edward Westley."

"Your photo proves nothing, only that I stopped in her office."

"We both know that you impersonated Beryl Westley and led Sophie to believe that the snakes were a harmless prank. You came to her office in disguise. You must have used stage make up. Look at that nose." Emily tapped the photo. "That's not your nose."

Clare bent over the photo and nodded. "You're right. This probably isn't me at all."

"You were positively identified. That's how I found you. You paid Sophie for her services. That money can be traced to you." Emily had no idea if this was true, but it sounded likely.

"I went to Sophie's office on perfectly legitimate business. I wanted to hire a temp worker to help me with publicity for this production. It's a time consuming, boring chore to be forever posting on social media. But it must be done."

Emily realized that the short walk from the theatre to the pub had given Clare enough time to come up with a plausible excuse. She looked confident now, with her story no doubt well-rehearsed in her head.

"Why were you disguised as Beryl Westley?"

Clare hooted. "You certainly don't think I look like Beryl Westley in that photo, do you? I have no idea what the woman looks like. I just didn't want to be recognized and pestered by my fans so I altered my appearance a bit."

Emily bit back the retort that was on the tip of her tongue; you're not exactly a famous rock star. Instead she asked, "Why would Sophie lie?"

"Perhaps she wanted to frame someone for the murder, and I was handy."

Emily switched tactics. "You were friends with Edward Westley when you were children, weren't you? What happened?"

"I don't have to answer your questions. Now that I know who you are and how little reason you have to trouble me, I'll finish my wine, which by the way is delicious, and then be off." Clare smiled and leaned back in her chair, perfectly at her ease. "Now, since it turns out you are actually a reporter, perhaps you'd like to talk about the play. We could use the publicity.

Tourists are our bread and butter. As it happens, I have a great deal more to say about Jacobean drama than about the ridiculous notion that I was behind some prank."

"Fine." Emily poised her pen over her notebook and looked at Clare with interest. "Is that because the Jacobean theme of revenge interests you?"

Clare took a sip of wine. "As a matter of fact, I do find revenge tragedies fascinating. Thomas Kyd lived in the age of Shakespeare when the state was taking over private citizens' role of revenging their relatives. Often justice did not prevail. Have you read the play?"

"Yes, in college. I was an English major. And then last night I skimmed through to refresh my memory."

"Then you know that my character Bel-Imperia seeks revenge for the murder of her lover. Justice has failed her. The killer is going to get away with murder and, to add insult to injury, her arrogant brother is trying to force her to marry the repulsive human being who killed her lover. In the scene we were rehearsing you saw Bel-Imperia stab the killer, then commit suicide. Revenge was satisfied."

Emily jotted down her remarks. "The plot clearly speaks to you. Why is that?"

"I beg your pardon." Clare's look of confusion was convincing. "I thought I had made myself perfectly clear."

"Readers like a personal angle. Are there any parallels in your own life? Any time when you had a good reason to seek revenge?"

Clare stood to her full height. "This interview is over. Good day."

Chapter 9

"It looks pretty bleak for Sophie," Emily said as she and Jack left the Garrick. "I think I made the situation worse. Now Clare has her story ready for the police. She knows what to expect."

"She would have come up with that story anyway. In fact, she probably had it in her back pocket just in case she was discovered." Jack put his arm around Emily. "You have tangled with a formidable woman."

"At least I'm not in traction in a National Health Service hospital, thanks to you, Jack." Emily leaned against him and gave him a quick kiss.

"Clare probably didn't mean to force you off the edge of the stage, but she did look menacing. Still in character perhaps."

"She was born to play Bel-Imperia. The vengeful one."

Jack chuckled. "I have to agree. Where to now, tour guide?"

"Let's head to Shakespeare's birthplace so I can start working on my article. It's right here in town and it will get us in a suitably Tudor mood."

"Right-ho, lead the way."

The house where Shakespeare was born was a handsome half-timbered Elizabethan building with a gable and mullioned windows. Emily and Jack bought combo tickets, which would admit them to five sites of interest, then stepped around the corner to a room where a montage of black-and-white photos of actors playing Shakespearean roles was projected on the wall. Disembodied voices recited well-known lines. "Be thou a spirit of health or goblin damned? Bring with thee airs from Heaven or blasts from Hell?" Hamlet's voice faded out. "Methought I heard a voice cry, sleep no more! Macbeth does murder sleep."

Emily felt immersed in the words of Shakespeare by the time a guide came to usher her and Jack into a garden, then into the house where Will was born. Upstairs they saw the bedroom where he had slept when he was a boy. The wallpaper had a bold black and white pattern that looked surprisingly modern.

"I didn't expect to see wallpaper in so old a house," Emily said.

The guide, wearing an Elizabethan doublet, was eager to explain. "The wallpaper was made of cloth to keep out the cold. Windows were another way to keep warm. They were so valuable that homeowners took them out when they left the house to prevent them from being stolen. Only the well-to-do could afford windows. They were taxed on the theory that if you could afford to warm your house, you must be wealthy enough to pay taxes."

Emily thanked him. She and Jack moved on to the next room to see the bed where Will was born. Another costumed guide greeted them. "Shakespeare's father, a glove maker and the mayor of Stratford, was wealthy enough to afford the biggest house on his street. Will was born in this bed, grew up, and lived here with his wife for the first five years of his marriage. He inherited the house after his father died." Emily was amazed that she was actually in the same room where Shakespeare drew his first breath and was treading on boards where he had once walked. She glanced at Jack to see if he was similarly awed. He seemed to be taking the experience more in stride.

As Emily and Jack went out into the garden, Emily turned to Jack. "You enjoyed the tour, didn't you?"

"I certainly did. You've taken me to so many of Shakespeare's plays that I've become interested in the guy."

"Good. I will definitely encourage my readers to come here." Emily whipped out her red notebook.

> ***Travelers' Tip***: *Stratford upon Avon is a dream come true for theater and history lovers. Here, the greatest English playwright was born in the half-timbered manor house where his father made elegant gloves. It feels like a real Elizabethan home, not a museum, and the costumed guides preserve the illusion. When you visit Shakespeare's birthplace, you'll feel as if you've stepped back in time; Will might walk in at any minute and join you.*

As Emily and Jack walked out into the busy street where students, herded by teachers, hustled along and tourists wandered, her thoughts returned to their encounter with Clare.

"Maybe it's the influence of Kyd's revenge play, but I wonder if revenge was Clare's motive. She pretended not to understand when I asked if that was why she was drawn to the role of Bel-Imperia. And she stonewalled when I asked about Edward and their relationship as children. Maybe her motive has something to do with the accident."

"Trevor told me that the decision to produce a Jacobean revenge drama was Clare's idea," Jack said. "She may be obsessed with vengeance."

"Shakespeare was interested in the topic too. Poor Hamlet, charged by his father's ghost to revenge his murder."

"Hamlet is a much more complex character than Bel-Imperia."

"True," Emily said. "I've always thought Hamlet was absolutely right to hesitate. How would he know if the apparition was a ghost or demon? Or if his uncle was really guilty? Shakespeare knew we're in the horrible position of having to act without knowing all the facts. We're limited by our own perceptions, by the influence of others, by our imagination. And murder is so final. You want to be sure you're right."

"I don't think Sophie was troubled by these doubts," Jack said.

"No. Perhaps she should have been. But I believe her. I think Clare is lying. I think she did hire Sophie to plant the snakes."

"Me too. But it will be hard to prove."

"I wish we knew if Clare meant to play a cruel prank or if she knew that Edward might die? Do you suppose he had a heart condition and she found out about it?"

"She's not going to tell us," Jack said.

"No. But maybe I can find out if she had a motive and how strong it was. I wonder if Bridey would tell me more about the accident. She was so excited about the Cheltenham race that our meeting was cut short, but she loves to gossip. I think I'll call her."

When Emily phoned her, Bridey burbled, "Oh of course I remember you, dearie. You brought me good luck. I'd be happy to meet you again. Kingsbridge Pub?"

And so, Emily found herself seated across from Bridey at the pub in Bourton-on-the-Water the next afternoon. Bridey ordered a Jameson Irish whiskey and ginger ale with a slice of lime.

"Just like a Big Ginger," Emily said, recognizing her favorite beverage at The Local, a fine Irish bar back home in Minneapolis. She ordered one too. Jack would drive home. He was once again shopping at the Country

Gentleman store in Chipping Campden and planned to swing by to pick her up in time for dinner.

"I was wondering about the accident that you said changed the relationship between Clare and Edward," Emily said to Bridey after they exchanged pleasantries and happy reminiscences of race day. "I read the newspaper account and noticed that it didn't name the driver. I wondered if it could have been Edward."

"Yes! That's just it! That's how the trouble between them started." Bridey slapped the table and leaned forward. "You guessed it so I don't have to feel guilty about spreading rumors. Edward's car hit Cyril and the poor lad died."

"Edward must have been just a boy. About sixteen? He was probably just learning to drive. Clare couldn't blame him, could she?"

"Oh, couldn't she just? And it was worse than that. Clare thought he killed her brother on purpose. The police believed it was an accident. Not Clare. I'll never forget how horrible and shocking it was. I was just putting away the dinner dishes when I heard a blood-curdling shriek, then a thump. I ran outside and saw a car stopped in the middle of the street and a body lying in a red pool that spread and oozed and ran down into the gutter. I screamed bloody murder. I couldn't help myself. And at the time I had no idea it was our Cyril lying in the street, his life's blood draining away. Clare was standing in front of the house, pale as a ghost, shivering, hugging herself."

"How horrible," Emily said.

"It was, it was." Bridey sighed. "I can hardly bear to think of it."

Emily thought Bridey's grief for the boy was real, but she clearly enjoyed telling the dramatic tale, one she had probably polished over the years. "I don't want to force you to relive such a painful experience," Emily said, "but if you don't mind, I'd like to know what happened next. Anything you recall could be helpful."

"Well, I'll just have to overcome me feelings." Bridey hauled out a large handkerchief and dabbed at her eyes. She heaved a great sigh and then launched into an account of Cyril's death that was enlivened by her apparently total recall of what was said.

"Later that night, a police officer drove Clare home from the hospital. Edward's car had been towed away and the blood mopped up, so the street looked as if nothing had happened. Edward was at the police station being questioned. Cyril's parents were still at the hospital. All that night, I had been praying that Cyril would pull through. But when Clare walked in the door.... oh I'll never forget how she looked! The minute I saw that girl's face I knew her brother was dead. 'Holy Mother of God!' I cried. 'You poor child. I'll pray for Cyril's soul. And for Edward. He must feel so guilty.' Clare looked at me as if she were carved out of stone. She didn't say a word.

"'What a terrible, tragic accident!' I said to her."

"'It was no accident,' Clare said in a voice cold as death."

"'What do you mean?' I asked her."

"'He did it on purpose. Edward meant to kill my brother. I saw it. I saw him speed up when he saw Cyril crossing the street. He aimed at him and mowed him down.'"

"'That can't be true. You're in shock. You don't mean it.'"

"'Every word. I told the officer who drove me home and he dismissed it out of hand, said Edward was a young boy, just learning to drive, maybe he hit the accelerator instead of the brake. It's inconceivable that he'd do it on purpose.'"

"'He's right, you know,' I told her."

"But Clare took no heed. She was never the same. The spark and joy went out of that girl. She never saw Edward again." Bridey took a reviving gulp of her Big Ginger and leaned back in her chair.

"How awful," Emily said. "Did Clare have any reason to think Edward would want to kill her brother? I know Cyril bullied him when they were children. Nanny Rose told me about the snake incident. And you told me that Cyril tried to keep Edward away from Clare. But surely these wouldn't be reasons enough for murder."

"No. I think something dreadful happened when the boys were up at Blanchley Hall. When they came down at the end of term, there was clearly bad blood between them. One afternoon, Edward was at the house chatting with Clare. When Cyril came in...oh you should have seen the look that passed between them. It would have frozen your blood. Edward clenched his fists, tightened his jaw. Tears stood in his eyes. He kept swallowing and staring at Cyril as if he hated him. Cyril looked frightened, which surprised me. He was always the bigger, stronger, dominant lad.

"'No hard feelings, right?' Cyril asked Edward."

"'Course, not,' Clare said. 'You don't have to worry, Cyril. Your precious secret's safe with Edward.'"

"'Good man.'"

"Edward left without looking at either of them or saying a word."

Bridey rattled the ice cubes in her empty glass and looked hopefully at Emily, who was glad to oblige.

When Jack pulled up in front of the Kingsbridge Pub, Emily had already said goodbye to Bridey and was waiting for him out front. She hopped into the Range Rover, and on the drive back to Stratford, told Jack what she had learned from Bridey. "The mystery deepens," she said. "Clare had a strong motive to want to harm Edward. Ever since she was a young girl, she's believed that he killed her brother on purpose. And yet, she waited until now to act. Why?"

Jack intoned, "I was angry with my friend; I told my wrath, my wrath did end. I was angry with my foe; I told it not, my wrath did grow."

Emily smiled. "Being able to quote William Blake right off the top of your head is impressive."

"One of my mom's favorite quotes," Jack admitted.

Emily laughed. "Still, you remembered it. Maybe your mom and Blake are right. Or maybe Clare has wanted revenge all this time and just found out that Edward had a heart condition and saw her chance to do real damage."

Emily's phone beeped. "Emily, now I know why the police want to arrest Sophie." As usual Vanessa plunged right in without any preliminaries. "The coroner's report was just released. He found that Westley was poisoned. He didn't die of snakebite or a heart attack. Now the police believe that it wasn't a prank gone wrong, but deliberate murder. And they assume Sophie is guilty."

"Good lord!" Emily cried.

"What is it?" Jack asked, swerving to avoid a hiker walking a border collie slowly across the road, which was flanked by tall hedges on each side.

Emily put the phone on speaker.

"I just added Jack. We're both stunned. Does Sophie have any reason to want Edward dead?"

"No, of course not. I know Sophie didn't poison Edward. She doesn't even know the man."

"Do you think Clare could have poisoned him and tried to frame Sophie?

"Maybe. But why?"

Emily told Vanessa about Clare's belief that Edward had murdered her brother.

"That's preposterous. I've never heard anyone say a negative word about Edward. He was a paragon of virtue. He would never have run over anyone on purpose. Clare must have imagined it."

"That's certainly possible. The police didn't believe her story."

"You have to find out where Clare was the night of Edward's murder," Vanessa said.

"Easier said than done. She's not very forthcoming."

"You can do it. I have great confidence in you."

Later that evening, Emily led the way to Edward Moon, a brasserie in the heart of Stratford. She knew Moon's was named for a chef who had worked in the British Colonial service in the early 1900s. He was famous in diplomatic circles for cooking traditional English dinners wherever he was posted and for using local ingredients in creative ways. The restaurant named after him follows that tradition and Emily was eager to try it.

Many paned windows trimmed with black gave the white building an elegant, old fashioned look, but inside Emily found that modern furniture and bright red walls created a vibe that was relaxed and welcoming. A chalk board listed their menu choices. Once they were seated and served their meal, Emily and Jack continued to discuss the mystery that absorbed them.

"So, are you going to tackle the formidable Clare again?" Jack took a bite of braised lamb shank. "Mmmm, this is delicious."

"Maybe. I do suspect her. She could have arranged to meet Edward at the hotel, ordered wine, and slipped poison into his glass."

"Would he be so quick to meet a woman who hated him?"

"He might have thought her offer to meet was a peace offering. If he still treasured his memory of their childhood friendship, he may have hoped Clare felt the same. He would have been eager to believe her." The story was neatly falling into place in Emily's mind.

"First off, we have to find out if Clare could have been in Chipping Campden that night," Jack said.

"True. I wonder if Trevor would let us see the rehearsal schedule. We might find out that way. I wouldn't believe Clare even if she said she wasn't anywhere near the hotel the night Edward was murdered. I think I'll go back to the theatre tomorrow and see what I can find out."

"One thing troubles me," Jack said. "How did the police know Sophie had planted the snakes in the first place?"

"An anonymous letter, remember?"

"Yes, of course, and that's an interesting point. Who do you suppose wrote that letter accusing Sophie? It wouldn't have been Clare Benson. She had every reason to keep it a secret so it wouldn't lead back to her."

"You're right. The police would never have thought of Sophie if it were not for the letter."

"Someone who worked in the hotel might have wanted to tip off the police without getting in trouble," Jack said.

"How would they know Sophie's real name? She was probably in disguise and was using an alias."

"Maybe someone was really targeting Sophie," Jack suggested. "This unknown person with a grudge against Sophie could have found out about the snake prank, poisoned Edward and then sent the anonymous letter to frame Sophie. Maybe Edward was just collateral damage."

"Possible, I suppose. But it calls for a cruel, callous disregard for human life."

"You hear of people bombing planes just to kill one person," Jack said. "There are ruthless people in this world."

Emily agreed. She was glad Jack was joining in her attempts to solve the murder. Her previous boyfriend had not been so helpful.

When Emily returned to the theatre the next day, she found the door unlocked, but no one answered when she yelled, "Halloo! Anyone here?"

In the lobby, Emily saw a rehearsal schedule posted on a corkboard and searched until she found the date of Edward's murder, March 13. "Full cast run through, 5 p.m. to 10 p.m."

The door to the auditorium opened and Trevor stared at Emily. "What are you doing here? Clare told me she had given you an interview, but she didn't think it would lead to much publicity."

"I was just checking your rehearsal schedule. Do you stick to it pretty closely?"

"Of course."

"Was Clare here all evening on March 13?"

"It says so, doesn't it?"

Trevor's cooperative spirit seemed to have faded. Emily wondered what Clare had told him. "Maybe you were rehearsing scenes Clare wasn't in," she suggested.

"Full cast means just what it says. Why do you care where Clare was that night?"

Clare flung open the door and stormed into the lobby. "Why? Because she thinks I killed Edward Westley?"

Emily wondered if she'd been waiting on the other side of the door for her cue. Apparently, she had given up trying to keep Trevor in the dark.

"I'm not accusing you of anything, Clare. I just want to rule you out. If you were here rehearsing—"

"Police rule people out. Not nosy parkers like yourself."

"Good point. And, trust me, the police will be on it. Did you see the news report about Edward being poisoned? This is serious. It's no longer a question of a prank gone wrong. It's deliberate murder. And Sophie will tell the police that you hired her."

"Not to poison anyone," Clare cried.

Emily realized that Clare must not have seen the news report. She looked genuinely shocked. "Just to frighten Edward?" Emily suggested.

"Not even that. I wanted him to feel as if the spirit of my brother Cyril was tormenting him. The snakes were just the sort of prank Cyril would have played. There was nothing wrong with Edward's heart. Not as far as I know. The snakes wouldn't have killed him, but they would have reminded him of what he'd done. Like a voice from the dead. The voice of the boy he murdered."

"You think Edward murdered Cyril?" Emily managed to sound surprised.

"I know he did. That's why I wanted to torment him. He ran over my brother with his automobile and the law did nothing. Nothing. Edward got away with murder.

"So, you were right. I did want revenge. Maybe I was influenced by the revenge tragedies we've been staging. I felt the spirit of the strong women I played rebuke me for letting my brother go unrevenged. It began to obsess me. I'd wake in the night wondering how I could get even.

"When I heard about Sophie's service, Vindi Cat, I thought it would bring me some relief. But Sophie would never have taken on a case if she knew it was so serious that I might want to physically harm Edward. She would have been suspicious of me. I knew that. She specialized in more subtle means of revenge, and that was fine with me."

"But snakes were subtle enough for her?"

"To tell the truth, Sophie didn't like it when I came up with the idea of the snakes. She wanted to be the one with all the ideas, so she didn't agree to my plan right away. I had to talk her into it."

"Why did you pretend to be Mrs. Westley?"

"I told you. I was afraid Sophie wouldn't take the case otherwise."

"And you made up the whole story about the family's practical jokes?"

"Yes. Complete fabrications. I excelled in my improv classes. I approached this the same way and quite enjoyed it."

"So, did you go to the hotel that night to see your plan in action?"

"No, I was in rehearsal."

"Yes, she was," Trevor said. "The whole cast will back us up."

"Good. Then you have nothing to worry about."

"Of course, I don't."

"Did you tell anyone about your plan, Clare? Someone you thought would find it amusing or gratifying in some way, someone who might have piggybacked on your idea, adding the deadly poison?"

"Certainly not."

"Someone knew about the snakes, the same person who wrote the anonymous letter about Sophie and sent it to the police. That letter leads to you. The police will be asking you questions."

"An officer called this morning," Trevor said.

Clare's actor face, which showed every subtle emotion, registered stark fear. Her eyes were wide, the veins in her neck distended, her breath shallow and rapid.

"Who was it?" Emily persisted. "You must have let something slip."

Clare paced the length of the lobby, her head high, not looking at her. Emily waited.

Finally, Clare wheeled around and drew a deep breath. "All right. I told Fiona. She's the girl who told me about Sophie and Vindi Cat to begin with. I knew she'd get a thrill out of hearing what I planned. She's that kind of girl."

"The kind of girl who would want to get Sophie in trouble?"

"Maybe. Fiona went to Sophie for help and Sophie turned her down. She resented it. That's why I knew I had to dissemble a bit if I wanted Sophie to take on my case."

"Where can I find Fiona?"

"She was our stage manager, but she quit a week ago."

"Where is she now?"

"I have no idea."

"I know," Trevor said. Clare shot him an angry look, but he ignored her. "I have her forwarding address in my office."

He turned to Clare. "I don't want you to take the blame for something Fiona may have done."

"Thank you," Emily said. "I'll just ask Fiona a few questions. Is she still here in Stratford?"

"No, she's working at Warwick Castle as a tour guide," Trevor said. "It's not far."

"Lots of failed actors end up there," Clare said. "Fiona tried to make it as an actor. She auditioned for roles here a number of times, but she just wasn't good enough. She didn't believe that, of course. There was always some reason someone had it in for her. She worked backstage for a while."

"I felt sorry for her," Trevor said. "She loved the theatre but didn't have much talent. It's a tough business, very competitive. Warwick is probably a good fit for her."

As Emily and Jack walked away from the theatre, following the path along the Avon, her phone belted out her newly chosen ring tone, a peal of bells." When Emily answered it, Vanessa sounded eager. "I can't wait to hear what you've found out. Come for tea and bring Jack. Today's school trip is to the stables. Jack can help Nigel with the ponies."

Emily agreed to join her. She and Jack were walking across the park toward the town of Stratford as she told Jack about Vanessa's invitation and her plans for him. "It's only a half-hour drive back to Chipping Campden so it will be an easy trip. Are you up for it?"

Jack tugged his forelock and shuffled his feet. "So, I'll be in the stables, will I? Muckin' out the ponies, while your ladyship'll be in the manor house, nibblin' on sweeties?"

Emily laughed. "I'm madly attracted to burly stable lads." She leaned against Jack and took his arm. "I do believe Vanessa will feel freer to talk openly if we are alone, which is why she wants you to help with kids on ponies."

Jack shuddered. "If you don't mind, I'll skip it. Nigel and his hound, along with hordes of small, sticky school children, are not tempting me. I'll kick around Stratford on my own and work on my article."

Chapter 10

That afternoon, at Chillingworth Manor, Emily joined Vanessa in the drawing room. An elderly maid brought a tray of cucumber sandwiches and scones. Emily was so intent on selecting one of the treats that she scarcely noticed the woman. She took a scone, spread on strawberry jam and clotted cream then took a bite. "Delicious. I'm becoming addicted to teatime."

The maid cleared her throat and leaned down to Vanessa. "Will you be wanting anything else, my lady?"

Emily recognized the voice. "Oh no, you fooled me again."

Sophie beamed at her.

"Do sit down, Sophie," Vanessa said. "It's my maid's day off," she explained to Emily. "No one will see her."

"I understand you've done a fine job of sleuthing, Emily. Tell me. What have you discovered?"

Emily launched into a recap of her discoveries, hoping the police would not interrupt her. "The false Beryl was played by Clare Benson, an actor and a childhood friend of Edward Westley. Clare believes he deliberately ran over and killed her brother Cyril when they were both teenagers even though the police dismissed the idea. Clare says she only meant to frighten Edward and remind him of his guilt so he would feel haunted by her brother. She told me she had no intention of causing a heart attack and certainly didn't poison him."

"If she's innocent, why did she impersonate Beryl and make up an elaborate story about pranks? Why not hire me as herself?"

"Clare says it's because you turned down her friend Fiona Simmons. She thought you'd turn her down too. Do you know what she was talking about?"

"I do remember Fiona. She's a very unstable woman. It's true that I wouldn't accept her as a client. She was too intense and angry. She didn't specify what she wanted me to do but I sensed she wouldn't rule out physical violence. I didn't know if she had a legitimate reason to seek revenge. Fiona wanted me to target the surgeon who had operated on her husband. She blames him for her husband's death. But I couldn't tell. Was he really at fault? Or was it just a bad outcome that couldn't have been prevented? Fiona didn't show me any proof that his hospital or his profession had disciplined him. It was too sketchy. I had a bad feeling about her."

"See. I told you Sophie was very scrupulous," Vanessa said.

Emily was surprised that Sophie drew the line somewhere.

"So maybe Clare was right," Sophie said. "There are parallels. Clare believes Edward killed her brother, but apparently there's no proof. I probably would have refused to take her on as a client if she had told the truth."

"No matter what she says, Clare must be the killer," Vanessa said. "You're in the clear, Sophie."

Emily hated to disillusion them. Both women looked giddy with relief.

"Excellent work, Emily," Vanessa said. Sophie nodded her approval.

"I wish it were so simple," Emily said slowly. "I too was sure that False Beryl was the killer and we only had to find her. But she can't be. Clare was in rehearsal all that evening. The director said the whole cast was present and could vouch for her."

"Do you believe him?" Sophie asked.

"It would be too easy for the police to check. So yes, I think he's telling the truth."

"We've come to a dead end," Vanessa said.

"Who else knew about the snakes?" Sophie asked.

"Exactly what I asked Clare," Emily said. "The only person she told was Fiona. Clare thought she'd get a kick out of it."

"Do you think Fiona could have been involved?" Vanessa asked.

"I don't know," Emily said. "Sophie, you said Fiona seemed unstable. How unstable? Clare said she was resentful that you helped other people but rejected her. Would she try to get even with you for that?"

"It's possible. I didn't see enough of her to form a considered opinion. Perhaps I was a bit abrupt with her."

"Why? Was she angry at you?"

"She was furious. I had to ask my staff to escort her from the building."

The clock chimed four times and Vanessa leapt to her feet. "Oh dear, Nigel will be here in a few minutes. If he knew you were here, Sophie, he'd be upset." She turned to Emily. "Would you mind terribly dropping Sophie off in town?"

"If you want to go to the police station, I'd be glad to do it," Emily said, well aware that this was unlikely to be the case.

"No, not yet," Sophie said. "I'll stay undercover for a little longer if you don't mind."

"I don't mind a bit as long as I'm not aiding and abetting. I really think you should tell the police what you know and let them get on with solving the case."

Sophie sighed. "Very well then. If you won't, you won't. I'll just clear away the tea things."

"No need," Vanessa said. "You're not really the maid."

"I like to stay in character." Sophie picked up the tray. She bent down and whispered a few words to Vanessa.

"Let's take a turn in the garden, before you go," Vanessa said to Emily. "I want to show you my David Austin roses."

Emily suspected Vanessa planned to work on her sympathies but, as it turned out, Vanessa didn't mention Sophie again. As they stood in the garden, she pointed across the field to the row of school children, leaving the stable, waving to Nigel and the groom.

"We never had such lovely field trips when we were little," Vanessa said, leading Emily into the rose garden. "This is my favorite rose," she said, cupping a white flower as fluffy and many petalled as a peony. It's called Glamis Castle after the setting for Macbeth and the home where Queen Elizabeth lived when she was a girl. It's quite fragrant."

Emily bent over the gorgeous rose and inhaled its unusual scent.

"It smells like myrrh or so I'm told," Vanessa said. "I have no idea what myrrh smells like, so I take that on faith."

"This has been lovely," Emily said, straightening up. "But I do have to get back to Jack."

"Of course." Vanessa hugged her. "Thank you for helping Sophie. It means a lot to me. Would you mind doing just one more small favor?"

"If I can."

"Just drop off a note at the bookstore in town. I'm requesting a new book."

"Sure." Emily was relieved it had nothing to do with Sophie for a change.

Emily climbed into the Range Rover and drove into the town of Chipping Campden. She handed Vanessa's note to the woman behind the desk in the small, cluttered bookshop and, resisting the temptation to browse among the dusty shelves, she headed back to the car.

To her horror, she heard banging coming from the trunk. Already sure of what she would find, she popped it open and looked down at the figure, dressed in black, curled into a fetal position.

"Thank God. I thought there was a latch in here. There's supposed to be."

"*You* are definitely *not* supposed to be here," Emily said through clenched teeth. "Get out. Go. That was a dirty trick. I'll never forgive Vanessa."

"She didn't know." Sophie unfurled herself and crawled out of the car. "It's damned cramped in the boot." She was wearing a nondescript black outfit —a hoodie and slacks. "I'll be going. I can catch a bus."

Emily looked around quickly, hoping they had not been observed as Sophie sidled away.

"I should have suspected something," Emily told Jack later when they were enjoying a pint of ale at the Garrick. She had just finished telling him about Sophie's unexpected appearance disguised as a maid and her comments about Fiona Simmons. "It wasn't like Sophie to give up without a fuss when I said I wouldn't drive her into town."

"I wish I had gone with you."

"Do you think you could have done better and prevented her from tricking us? I doubt it. She was very convincing,"

Jack covered her hand with his. "Probably not. I would have liked to try though."

"You would have been in the stables, remember?"

Jack laughed. "Too true. Tell me more about Sophie's opinion of Fiona. Is she our new suspect?"

"Possibly. I'd like to ask her a few questions. Maybe we should go to Warwick Castle. I can easily work it into my article."

"I thought you were going to feature Blenheim Palace. Surely you don't need two castles."

"Warwick will work just as well, and it's closer. As you know, I'm telling my readers about easy day trips from London."

"I'm sticking with you this time," Jack said taking a swig of Guinness.

Emily didn't admit it, but she was pleased that she would not be alone with an unstable woman who may have killed Edward Westley.

Chapter 11

During the eight-mile drive from Stratford to Warwick Castle, Emily gave Jack the benefit of her research. "Warwick Castle is the most magnificent medieval castle in England. It was built by William the Conqueror in 1068. Since then it gradually changed from an imposing fortress to an elegant home with gardens designed by Capability Brown. Now it offers a unique historical experience to the public."

"You sound like a tour guide."

"I'm thinking about my article and practicing on you. I'm excited to see it. Vanessa told me she was inspired to save Chatsworth Manor by the success of the events at Warwick. It's managed by Merlin Entertainments and offers jousting, sword fights, falconry shows, history reenactments, the works."

"Like the Renaissance Fair in Minnesota."

"Yes, but on a much grander scale since all these events occur in a fabulous castle that is open all year round."

After parking the car, Emily and Jack walked through a tunnel of branches that twined into an archway overhead, then crossed a bridge over a grassy moat and finally reached the castle. Emily's heart thrilled when she looked up at the stone towers and turrets. The castle brought back memories of her favorite childhood stories about knights, chivalry, heroism and honor. She had loved to read about sword fights and jousts, Robin Hood, Sir Lancelot, King Arthur, the Three Musketeers.

"Oh, it is gorgeous," Emily said. "My nieces would love it."

"Apparently so do all the kids running around yelling," Jack said.

"We should find Fiona before we start exploring. Trevor said she's a tour guide so it should be easy to track her down."

They walked into the castle courtyard and headed for the entrance to the castle where a placard announced tours beginning at 11 a.m. and 2 p.m. They decided to return in a half hour.

After a quick exploration of the castle, Emily stopped to jot in her red notebook.

> *Travelers' Tip: Warwick Castle is a fabulous place for a family outing. Children will learn about British history as they make their way through a maze, explore an exhibit showing Richard Neville, Kingmaker, preparing for battle, and climb the ramparts and towers. Older children will enjoy being scared out of their wits in Castle Dungeon.*

When they returned to the castle entrance, Emily saw a slight woman with a sprinkle of freckles across her sharp nose and frizzy auburn hair standing beside the sign announcing tours. A small crowd had already gathered. "Are you Fiona Simmons?" Emily asked.

"Yes. How did you know? Have I met you?" Fiona leaned forward, squinting at Emily's face, trying to place her.

"Clare Benson told us you'd give an amazing tour of the castle," Emily enthused. "I'm so glad you're on duty today."

Fiona's pale skin flushed. "Clare said that, did she? Well, I hope this lives up to your expectations."

"This is Jack Flynn," Emily said. "We're traveling together." She hated to say 'boyfriend'. It sounded as if they were teenagers plus it gave more information than she wanted to share with a casual acquaintance.

"Well, good. Glad to have you with us. We'll just wait a few minutes before starting the tour." Fiona tapped her foot and hugged her notebook close to her chest. A group of about fifteen tourists ranging from an elderly couple to a young man and woman with an infant in a front pack and a toddler in a stroller were gathered around her.

Exactly at 11 a.m., Fiona led the group into the castle's Great Hall, a huge gallery filled with a dazzling display of armor for men and horses. The children in the group were enchanted. Emily nudged Jack. "Tiffany and Brittany would be ecstatic. They love knights on horseback." Her nieces were six and eight years old.

"Warwick Castle has been at the center of English history since the Norman Conquest in 1068," Fiona told them. "Here are just a few of the historical highlights. Warwick, the Kingmaker, once held two rivals for the crown as prisoners in its towers. King Richard III remodeled the castle, adding the Bear and Clarence towers. Queen Elizabeth I stayed here, battles in the War of the Roses and the English Civil War were fought here, and Oliver Cromwell used it as a prison.

"Our tour today will focus on the staterooms," Fiona continued. "During the Restoration, the state apartments were remodeled to reflect the splendor of that era."

She led them into a succession of gorgeous rooms illustrating the castle's history from medieval times to the 19th century. Eerily lifelike wax figures formed tableaux that brought history to life. Emily's favorite featured Henry VIII and all his unfortunate wives apparently having a grand reunion.

Finally, Fiona led them into the Secrets and Scandals of the Royal Weekend Party. "Here is where the Marlborough House Set, led by Bertie, Prince of Wales, partied during Victorian times," Fiona explained. "Daisy Maynard, Countess of Warwick, had an affair with Bertie, who later became King Edward VII." The wax figure of Daisy was shown at her dressing table preparing for a party. "She was the most beautiful woman in England and an avid ghost hunter. Daisy held séances in this very room." Fiona shivered and looked around the room. "Some say it is still haunted. Daisy raised the dead and they still linger."

Emily suspected that Fiona might be serious.

In the next room, a waxy young Winston Churchill and the future King Edward lounged before the fireplace.

"Listen carefully and you can hear the song, "Daisy, Daisy, give me your answer true," a tune written for the Countess, playing in this room."

Jack nudged Emily. "How do you suppose our Lily felt about Daisy sharing her royal lover?"

Emily had done her research. "Lily really couldn't complain. She had a baby with another man while she was carrying on with the prince. Besides I think Bertie's affair with Lily was over by the time he took up with Daisy. He had affairs with lots of married women, much to the horror of his mother, Queen Victoria."

Fiona frowned at her. "Shall we move into the hallway? You'll see some fascinating photos."

After the tour, Fiona said, "I hope you enjoyed it."

"Very much. I wonder if you have a few minutes to talk to us. Perhaps a cup of tea?"

Fiona drew back. "I'm working, as you can see."

"Surely not right this minute. The next tour isn't until 2 p.m. Clare spoke so highly of you that I've been eager to meet you."

Fiona looked wary. "How do you know Clare?"

"We stopped by Another Stage Theatre to watch a rehearsal of *The Spanish Tragedy*, I'm writing about it for the *Twin Cities Daily News*. Clare told me you're an actor so your tour would be especially entertaining. She was right."

Fiona smiled, apparently reassured by Emily's explanation.

"Do you have many opportunities to use your acting talents here?" Emily asked.

"I hope to be cast as one of the Witches of Warwick in *Castle Danger* or perhaps in another role that interests me."

"Marvelous. I'd love to hear more about it. Do you have time to talk?"

Fiona wavered. "I suppose I could take a break."

Emily realized that anyone who viewed Fiona as an actor had a bit of leverage.

"Perhaps you would join me in climbing the tower," Fiona said. I need to get my exercise. There are 530 steps so it's quite good for us."

"Yes, excellent," Jack said. Emily knew he was missing his regular workouts.

"I'll show you where the Castle ghost jumped to her death. I hope to play her part in a reenactment at some point. It really needs an actor in the role, not just some random docent." Fiona led the way up steep, winding steps and along the windy rampart where children were pretending to shoot longbows.

At the top of Caesar's Tower, the view of the castle courtyard and the hills beyond was spectacular. Fiona turned to them, her hair whipping behind her, holding it back with one hand. "So, do you want to hear about the ghost?"

"Yes, of course," Emily said.

"During the Middle Ages, Moll Bloxham was stealing bread and ale from the castle and selling it in town. When the Earl of Warwick found out what she was doing, he banned her from the castle. Moll was furious. In revenge, she put a curse on him and everyone in the castle. It became clear she was a witch. Warwick arranged for priests to perform exorcisms on her, but she was too powerful. Finally, Moll was chased up here to Caesar's Tower where she jumped into the River Avon. Her body was never found. You see she had changed into a huge, black dog. Howls are still heard in the castle." Fiona looked agitated, leaning over the parapet, apparently stirred by her own tale.

"I suppose most ancient castles have their ghosts. That's a particularly good one," Jack said.

"Don't be so dismissive," Fiona snapped. "Many people believe that Moll is a living witch, who can appear as a dog or project her evil spirit back into Warwick Castle. I myself have heard her howls."

Jack chuckled. "If I heard howling, I'd guess it was a local dog baying at the moon."

Emily dug her elbow into his side and shot him a sharp look. If interest in ghost stories was the price of hearing what Fiona had to say, she was willing to pay. They walked along the rampart and descended the narrow winding steps. When they reached the bottom, Emily turned to Fiona, "Shall we have a cup of tea?"

"I don't have time for tea, but we can walk toward the Peacock Garden. Daisy brought peacocks here and they've been here ever since. Birds as beautiful as she was."

"Good." Emily felt that Fiona was relaxed, and the time was right to introduce the topic on her mind. "As a reporter, I've been following the strange story about the MP who was murdered," she said as they walked along. "At first, the newspaper articles suggested he was killed by snake bites, then that he was frightened into having a heart attack and now he seems to have been poisoned."

Fiona looked uncomfortable. "Poisoned? Really? I hadn't heard that." She kept walking, head down, her fingers kneading the fabric of her skirt.

"I was fascinated by the inside story Clare told me," Emily continued. "She said she hired Sophie Morton to play a prank on Edward Westley, in fact, to put snakes in his bed. Emily stopped and shot a look at Fiona's impassive face. "But you know that, don't you? Clare told you because she thought you'd get a kick out of it."

"Why would I care? I don't know Edward Westley."

"No, but you were certainly interested in Sophie. Clare told me that Sophie was willing to help her, but not you."

"That's right. It didn't surprise me though. Somehow Clare always gets everything she wants. Sophie would never say no to her. Nobody does." Fiona's pale face was rigid with resentment. "When I auditioned for a major role at Another Stage, I was cast as a lady in waiting. Can you imagine? Not even a speaking part. Basically, a maid."

Emily made a sympathetic sound. "Clare told me you had a good reason to want Sophie to help you."

"That's right. Doctor Shore murdered my husband."

Emily managed to gasp as if hearing this for the first time. "Really? He killed him?"

"Probably not on purpose. But after Shore operated on him for pancreatic cancer, my Kevin never recovered. He lingered for a month and then he died."

"Sometimes patients do die despite our best efforts," Jack said. Emily put a silencing hand on Jack's arm. She knew he wanted to plunge in and defend the unknown doctor.

"How horrible for you to lose your husband," Emily said. "I'm sorry."

"It was heartbreaking. Kevin was only thirty-three. Too young to die. Dr. Shore couldn't have done his job properly. I told Sophie he deserved to have something horrible happen to him. She asked me what I had in mind. I said, 'Use your imagination. What would be the worst thing that could happen to a doctor?' I knew she had come up with very appropriate revenge schemes for other women. Why not for me?"

"Did she say why she refused you?

Fiona ignored the question. "I tossed out a few suggestions. Not specifying exactly what I wanted but giving ideas since apparently Sophie didn't have any of her own." Fiona sniffed.

"Such as?"

"An accident that smashed his hand so he couldn't operate would be good. Or some trauma to the head that left him slightly brain damaged."

Jack was simmering. "Really? Such extreme measures against a doctor who may have been quite competent?"

Fiona snapped at him. "No, he wasn't competent. Obviously. Or my husband would be alive."

"How did Sophie react?" Emily, asked, nudging the conversation back on track.

"Sophie said she wouldn't do anything that caused physical harm. I said, 'Fine, what can you do to him?' She just shut down. Said she couldn't take the case. She looked at me as if I were some slug that she found under a rock."

"No wonder you wanted the police to know what she did to Edward Westley."

"What! I never said that."

"No. But you must have written the anonymous letter to the police accusing Sophie."

"Who told you that?"

"You were the only one Clare told."

"Don't believe everything she says."

"It's nothing to be ashamed of. You were just being a good citizen, giving the police information they needed. How did you know Edward was afraid of snakes?"

"Clare told me. She said he was a sniveling little coward who would get what was coming to him."

Fiona seemed to realize too late she had all but admitted writing the letter. Emily plunged on quickly before she could backtrack. "You shouldn't be afraid of the publicity. An actor's name should be out there, in front of the public."

Fiona hesitated. "Perhaps you're right. I didn't do anything wrong. Just tried to help."

"Exactly. I think you should go to the police and tell them everything you know."

"Then they'd find out about Clare."

"True. Is that a problem? Do you owe Clare any favors?"

"Not really. She's always been the queen bee. When we were at the RA, I was relegated to minor parts. She was usually cast as a queen with me walking behind, carrying her velvet train. How she lorded it over us all! It's her looks more than her talent that sets her apart, I believe."

"What do you plan to do?"

"I'm not sure. I'll think about it. Now I have to get back to work." She sneered at Jack and smiled at Emily as she hurried away across the courtyard.

"Have you had enough history for today?" Jack asked, "or do you want to persist in finding the peacocks?"

"I'm about ready to leave, but we should stop in the gift shop. I want to get presents for Tiffany and Brittany. At their age, I would have loved the armor and swords, but I believe they're into princesses now."

"Good. Dresses will fold up better. Otherwise you'd have to wear a plastic helmet on the plane."

As they headed back toward the gift shop, Jack asked, "Do you think Fiona could have poisoned Edward to get back at Sophie? Even if she didn't have anything against Edward?"

"It's possible. She's seething with resentment against Sophie and the doctor and she's jealous of Clare. She's awash in negativity. But I still think Clare is the more likely suspect from a psychological point of view. She has a powerful motive. It's too bad she has an iron-clad alibi."

"Is that why you were prodding Fiona to go to the police?"

"Exactly. I was hoping the police could figure out a way that Clare could have done it."

"A slow acting poison perhaps?"

"Maybe. I don't know what poison was actually given, but the police will know."

"Let's hope Fiona goes to them."

Emily called her sister Fanny and encouraged her to bring her daughters to Warwick Castle, which she described in vivid detail.

Fanny's reaction was enthusiastic. She was always a good audience for her sister. "It sounds absolutely wonderful! I wish I could pack up the girls and join you."

"Do it. Jack and I would love to see you."

"I couldn't really."

"The girls would have so much fun and it could spark a real interest in British history."

"Well, maybe, but British history isn't in their lesson plans. And we're totally booked this spring. The girls are in school now, then during spring break they have ballet lessons, and soccer and a piano recital.

You'll understand when you have kids of your own. Your life won't be quite so spontaneous."

"Another time then. When you can plan ahead. Good talking to you, Fanny. I have to get back to writing my article."

"Wait. Before you go. Emily, have you talked to Mom lately? She's working herself into a frenzy over your wedding. She's desperate for you to set a date."

Emily laughed. "She told me. I can't imagine why she's so eager when her own marriage was a disaster. Mom and Dad were miserable together. Their divorce was a blessed release."

"Oh, Emmy, no. Most of the time they were very happy."

"I don't remember that. I recall horrible fights. You just slept through them. They were late at night, after a few too many beverages."

"I know it was pretty bad at the end. But don't you remember how they used to laugh and joke around. Remember camping up North, the cabin near Gooseberry Falls where we went hiking, canoeing, and fishing. Remember Dad grilling the little sunfish we caught and Mom laughing because they were so small that we had to eat heaps and heaps. And our trip to Disneyland. Pizza on the porch Friday nights. Movie night with popcorn. Board games." Fanny was building up steam.

"Well, yeah. You're right. They did have fun sometimes." The ending had eclipsed Emily's happy memories. "Sometimes I was afraid they were going to kill each other. They were so violent."

"They were just dramatic. They both liked to throw plates and glasses and yell, but they never hit each other."

"Really?"

"I'm older than you are so maybe I remember more happy times, before it all fell apart. Don't let Mom and Dad's experience stand in your way."

"Of course not. I'm just surprised Mom is so keen on marriage."

Chapter 12

The following day, Emily and Jack immersed themselves in the history of Stratford by joining a walking tour that met at the fountain in the center of town.

Jack's interest in drama and history was a happy surprise. Emily would have loved him if he never read anything but medical journals and watched only talk shows on TV. After all, he made her laugh, he was trustworthy, clever, and sexy. His shared interests were like an unexpected gift and, after all, not so surprising. They had both grown up in Minneapolis, going to the Children's Theatre when they were small then graduating to the Guthrie Theater where they saw classic dramas from all eras including the Elizabethan. Jack had confessed his favorites were the bloody battle scenes, anything involving swords, shipwrecks, and mayhem, all scenes where a doctor's services would soon be required.

Their brisk enthusiastic tour guide walked quickly, stopping every now and again to give historical insights. She paused at a busy corner to explain that some buildings from Shakespeare's time are still standing and sometimes it's hard to tell them from newer buildings. Pointing across the street, she asked, "Which of those two half-timbered buildings do you think is Tudor?"

"That one." Jack said, pointing to the one on the left.

"Correct." She beamed at her apt pupil. "You probably spotted the uneven beams. In Tudor times, buildings were constructed of green oak, which would settle and bend."

"I noticed another clue," Jack said. "The plaque on the front of the other building says 1979."

"That too." The tour guide chuckled. "Hardly anybody notices that."

"Looks like you're teacher's pet now," Emily said, squeezing his arm.

They walked through town then paused before a large half-timbered building. "Across the street you'll see the school where Shakespeare studied Latin, read the poems of Ovid, and acted in plays by Terence, Sophocles and other classical playwrights. It is still a school, still free, and still teaches Latin. Boys must take an exam to be admitted.

"Shakespeare's father previewed plays for Queen Elizabeth at the school and decided whether or not to approve them. Will probably tagged along. He would have seen lots of plays and known actors who were probably helpful when he decided to go on the stage himself."

"I will definitely recommend this tour," Emily whispered to Jack. "This is fascinating," Jack agreed.

The tour group walked on through town to the house where Shakespeare had lived with his wife and children. As Emily gazed at the half-timbered buildings and crooked streets, she could picture this town in Elizabethan England, not so very different from now. A rip in time and she could catch a glimpse of Shakespeare as he strode along in doublet and hose, muttering to himself, rehearsing or composing. Here the Avon still flowed, and swans drifted along, as they must have in Tudor times.

Their tour concluded in Holy Trinity Church. In front of the altar, their tour guide pointed out Shakespeare's bust. "It was made from his death mask, so it shows him as he really looked—a fine looking man even in death." Emily thought he looked too ordinary. She would have preferred a more dashing countenance.

The tour guide read aloud the famous quote inscribed on his grave in front of the altar. "'Good friend for Jesus sake forebear to dig the dust enclosed here. Blest be the man that spares this stone and curst be he who moves my bones.' This gravestone stymied efforts to move Shakespeare's grave to Westminster Abbey. Shakespeare had the last word," the tour guide said.

Emily thanked her for an excellent overview of the Shakespearean town and its history. As she and Jack walked down to the river, her phone pinged.

"Emily, how are you?" It was Vanessa.

"Cross actually," Emily snapped. "I told you I didn't want to take Sophie into town."

"You didn't. She went off on her own."

"Nonsense. How could she? You must have been her accomplice."

"What do you mean?

"When I got to the bookstore—where you sent me—I heard a terrific banging from inside the trunk and who do you suppose was inside?"

"Not Sophie? Oh, no. I had no idea. I didn't help her, I swear. I knew nothing about it. How do you suppose she did it? How could she get your car keys?"

"Well, I must admit, I tossed them on the table in your hall out of habit. It's what I do at home."

"There you are then. Sophie helped herself to your keys, opened the trunk, and put your keys back while we were in the garden. I had nothing to do with it."

Emily was still suspicious. "Did Sophie ask you to lure me into the garden?"

"Hardly *lure*. She did suggest you would enjoy seeing the roses, but I had no idea it was part of a plot."

"Have you noticed how devious Sophie is?"

Vanessa was silent.

"Where do you think Sophie is now?"

"She's gone to ground. I haven't heard from her."

Emily felt her irritation melting away as she realized that her own carelessness with the keys had been part of the problem. "Vanessa, I talked to Fiona, the woman who Sophie suspected wrote the anonymous letter accusing her of deliberately trying to kill Westley by frightening him to death. Sophie was right. Fiona admitted it. I tried to convince her to go to the police."

"Do you think she will?"

"Maybe. If she does, the police are bound to ask her how she knew about Sophie planting the snakes and they'll get her to admit that Clare told her she had hired Sophie."

"Is Fiona as unstable as Sophie thought?"

"She's definitely an angry woman. She's angry at Sophie and jealous of Clare. I can see why Sophie wouldn't want to get involved with her."

"Emily, let's meet at The Black Swan. It's a lovely inn. Lunch will be my treat. Bring Jack. I hate to think of you being annoyed with me. I'm sorry I didn't see through Sophie's plan."

Only after she'd ended the call, did Emily realize that The Black Swan was the Inn where Edward was murdered. Vanessa probably had more than lunch in mind. Emily shared her suspicion with Jack.

"Well, at least, Vanessa is stepping up to the plate instead of just handing out instructions. I'm included in the lunch instead of being sent to the stable or somewhere similar."

"I wonder if I could find out anything useful if I talked to the staff at The Black Swan," Emily said.

"Like what?"

"Like who was at the Inn that night. We know that Beryl, Edward's real wife was there. But when did she arrive and when did she look into Edward's room? And, was Clare there—then or on a previous evening? We know Sophie was at the inn, but was she recognized?"

"Sounds like quite a crowd."

At noon, they parked in front of a gray stone building covered with ivy where twin lions crouched by the door and wood smoke curled from the chimney. Emily and Jack pushed open the heavy door and followed the hallway to a dining room where candles flickered on the tables and a fire blazed in the hearth. Vanessa was seated near the window. She rose as they came in.

"How lovely to see you both."

After exchanging warm greetings, they ordered lunch. Then Emily whispered, "I'm going to just slip upstairs for a moment."

Vanessa patted her hand. "Good for you, Emily."

"Don't get caught," Jack said.

Emily climbed the stairs to the second floor where she saw a woman in a black uniform vacuuming the hall. She turned off the machine for a moment and adjusted it.

Emily, pretending to be a tourist with a ghoulish interest in crime, said, "This is the hotel where the murder took place, isn't it?"

"I'm sure I don't know what you mean. I'm busy. I'm hoovering." The woman turned on the vacuum and set to work.

Emily turned back and walked up to the third floor where she paused in front of a room secured with yellow police tape. A broad faced woman with her hair in a net, walked toward her, pushing a cart of linens. "Looking for your room, dearie?"

"No. I was just thinking how hard it must have been for you—having a murder occur in this lovely old inn. You've probably never had a scandal here before."

"Oh, haven't we? You'd be surprised."

"Were you working the night it happened?"

"Sorry, miss. We've been told not to say a word to anyone about the incident."

"I understand." Emily held out a Cadbury fruit-and-nut bar with a ten-pound bill tucked beside it. "A snack for later?"

The woman looked at it and chuckled. "Aren't you a sly boots? What do you want to know?"

Emily pulled out her phone with the photo of Beryl. "Did you see this woman the night of the murder?"

"Certainly. That's Mrs. Westley. She comes here for lunch from time to time."

"When did you first notice her that night? Did she go into her husband's room?"

The woman tucked the bill into her pocket and paused.

"I'm helping the police with their inquiries," Emily assured her. She believed this was true, even though the police were unaware of her efforts and would probably advise her to cease and desist if they did know.

The woman's brow cleared. "Oh, that's different. Let me think. It was evening when she looked into her husband's room for the first time. Maybe 9 o'clock. Then, of course, about 5 a.m., when she found the body and holy hell broke loose. As it happened, I was working the late shift. Some of our guests like to have meals or snacks taken up to their rooms. I saw Mrs. Westley in the hallway. She turned to me and asked if Mr. Westley's guest had arrived yet.

"I said, 'No. Did you ask at the front desk?'"

"'I don't imagine his guest will bother with the front desk,' Mrs. Westley said. 'She's much more likely to sneak up the stairs and knock to be let in. I thought you might have noticed her.' Mrs. Westley looked furious, white faced, her jaw clenched. She used her cardkey to open the door to her husband's room and looked inside. She quickly shut the door and muttered, 'Not here yet.' I think she had forgotten I was standing there."

"Did you tell the police?" Emily asked.

"No. The management told us not to volunteer any information."

"Why do you think she was lurking in the hallway instead of joining her husband in his room?"

"I couldn't say."

Emily peeled off another ten pounds. "Did she seem shocked or surprised by what she saw in the room?"

"No. A little let down. This is just guessing, mind. But she looked ready for battle. I reckon that Mrs. Westley believed her husband was planning to meet a lover and she came here to confront them. When she opened that door, she expected to see him with some bit of fluff but either he was alone or the room was empty."

"Not likely there were snakes there then?"

"No. When she saw the snakes, it was much later. And did she scream!"

"You were here when she found the body then?"

"Yes, I was just about to go off duty. I heard a tremendous commotion and came running. Mrs. Westley was screaming. The door was open, and I could see inside. Snakes were crawling over the dead body. Horrible it was!"

A woman in a crisp, dark suit came bustling down the hallway, calling out, "Betty, who are you talking to?"

"This lady was lost. I was helping her find her way."

"That's right," Emily said. "She's been very helpful."

The suit didn't look convinced.

Emily came back to the dining room to find Vanessa and Jack scooping up the last of their soup.

"I asked them to hold yours. What did you find out?" Jack asked.

Emily told them.

"So, Beryl could have killed her husband," Vanessa said.

"Yes. She was at the inn and she had a motive. She thought Edward was being unfaithful and seemed furious."

"How would she have poisoned Edward?" Jack asked. "And how would she have known about the snakes?"

"Maybe she did see the snakes the first time she opened the door and saw her chance," Emily said. "She could have sneaked into the room again without being seen and added poison to his water glass or to some beverage he couldn't resist. Maybe he carried a flask and she knew it."

"It's not every wife that keeps poison in her purse in case her husband transgresses," Jack said.

Chapter 13

The next morning, Emily and Jack walked through the rain, holding aloft an umbrella emblazoned with the design of the red, white and blue British flag. "How embarrassing to go to a funeral looking as if we're in a parade," Emily said to Jack. She had lost her brolly and replaced it with a flamboyant umbrella from a tourist shop. Surrounding them was a sea of dark figures holding somber black umbrellas, plodding toward St. James, the village church in Chipping Camden, which they had visited the previous week.

"Maybe we should peel off and fade away," Jack said.

With the rain pitter pattering overhead and coldly dripping down the back of her neck, Emily was tempted by his suggestion, but resisted it. "Vanessa asked me to go to the funeral. She needs moral support."

"Why is Vanessa going if she thinks it will be so stressful that she needs your support?"

"Apparently, she and Nigel should be seen here for political reasons. "Lots of Westley's political friends and foes are here, I suppose. Luckily, this church is big enough to hold us all."

"It's not surprising that the funeral of an MP, who was murdered in such a sensational way is drawing a crowd," Jack said.

Emily agreed.

At the church door they stopped, and Jack shook rain from their gaudy umbrella. Emily was glad to see it furled. "So appropriate to have gloomy weather for a funeral," Jack said. "If it were sunny, you'd think it a shame the dear departed was missing it."

"He's missing it in any case, poor soul." Emily shot Jack a reproving look for his lighthearted remark.

"No doubt you're curious to see who will show up. Killers are notoriously unwilling to skip the funeral of their victims. Wanting to make sure they're dead, I suppose."

"I do wonder who will be here," Emily admitted.

The lugubrious, low notes of an organ pulsed through the church as they joined Vanessa and Nigel in a pew in the middle of the crowded church. Vanessa gave Emily a grateful look and patted her hand. As Emily looked over the congregation, somber in black and gray, a soprano launched into a particularly shrill rendition of, "The Day Thou Gavest Lord is Ended."

The vicar intoned, "Most merciful God, surround the family of Edward Westley with your love that they may not be overwhelmed by their loss, but have confidence in your goodness and strength to meet the days to come."

Emily glanced at Beryl Westley, sitting in the front pew on the other side of the aisle. She did not seem overwhelmed by loss but perfectly composed, her face a marble mask. Was she a dignified woman in control of her emotions, or just not overwhelmed by grief? Impossible to tell.

After the traditional liturgy of eulogies, prayers and hymns, the vicar brought the service to a close. "Holy Lord, hear our prayers as we entrust to you Edward Westley as you summon him out of this world. Forgive his sins and failings and grant him peace."

The vicar turned to the congregation, his hands upraised and said, "You are all welcome at the home of the deceased. Your presence will be a comfort to the bereaved."

Startled, Beryl Westley leapt to her feet, as if ready to insist he take back his invitation. But the service was over, the vicar's back turned, the organ was playing Mendelssohn's G Major Prelude.

"I wonder why he had to bring up sins and failings," Vanessa whispered as they slowly made their way back down the aisle. "It only makes people wonder."

"Hmmm. Did you see how surprised Beryl was that we were all invited back to her home?"

"I imagine she was planning a much more select gathering. The vicar is getting on in years. I believe he just blurted out what he usually says."

"Are you going?"

"Wouldn't miss it."

"Vanessa, are you sure we need to be there?" Nigel asked, clinging to a faint hope of a reprieve. "I have a good deal to do at home."

"You haven't really, you know. Besides, everyone would notice if you didn't go." She settled the matter, "Heaven knows what they would read into your absence."

Sophie in a long black cloak, wearing a broad-brimmed hat with a net veil covering her face, was edging her way toward them. She took Vanessa's arm as they walked out of the church.

"I felt I should pay my respects. That's why I came. Of course, the police are here too. Bound to be." Sophie scanned the people milling around in front of the church. "I see they've already spotted me."

"Why did you come here if you knew the police would arrest you?" Vanessa asked.

"I have to clear my name. I'm ready to answer their questions now. I am innocent so I have nothing to worry about." Sophie watched the officers moving toward her. "I hate to miss the gathering back at the house though. All Edward's supporters and well-wishers drinking Beryl's sherry and remembering what a fine fellow he was."

Emily was surprised to hear the edge of hostility in her voice. The stress of being a suspected murderess seemed to be wearing her down.

"Beryl wouldn't have wanted me there anyway," Sophie said. "So awkward now that she claims to be the heartbroken widow."

"You don't think she is?" Emily asked.

"She's a suspect, isn't she? Beryl was at the Inn the night Edward died. I saw her. Of course, I didn't know who she was at the time, but I remember her lurking around the hall."

"A maid told me Beryl looked into her husband's room twice," Emily said. "Once early in the evening when she seemed disappointed at what she saw—or didn't see—and the final time when she raised an outcry."

"So, not very heartbroken. You'll keep looking into it, won't you?"

"The police will, I'm sure. The maid thought Beryl expected to find Edward with a lover."

"Do the police know that?"

"Maybe not. You could tell them. I think you'll be spending some time in their company." Emily recognized the tall police officer who stepped in front of Sophie and held out his badge. "You'll remember me, Miss Morton. Sgt. Collin Norville of the Gloucestershire Constabulary."

"Yes, I remember you."

"In the light of new information, I'd like you to come to the station again to help with our inquiries into the death of Edward Westley." It didn't sound like an invitation she could refuse.

Sophie nodded and held out her wrists.

"That won't be necessary," the officer said. He turned toward Emily and Jack. "You're friends of Miss Morton, the ones who brought the flash drive."

"Acquaintances," Jack said.

"Ah." He turned to see that Vanessa and Nigel had faded into the crowd. "What happened to your other friends?" he asked Sophie.

"I don't really know them."

"Huh." He led her away from the church.

As soon as the officer and Sophie left, Vanessa and Nigel reappeared. "What a shame," Vanessa said.

"Where did you go?"

"I'd just as soon we didn't attract the attention of the police, thank you very much," Nigel said.

Vanessa sighed, "Poor Sophie."

Emily did not join in her lament. She was relieved that Sophie wouldn't be popping up when she least expected her and trying to inveigle her into aiding and abetting. But she kept this opinion to herself.

After a short drive, Emily and Jack pulled up in front of the house of the murder victim where his wife Beryl now lived alone. The Cotswold stone house with its thatched roof and roses growing in profusion over the doorway looked like an illustration from a tourist brochure.

Inside the crowded drawing room, Emily and Jack saw Beryl standing against the wall, a glass of wine in hand. Appropriately for a grieving widow, she wore a simple black dress. "Thank you for coming," she repeated automatically to guests as they walked by. Jack and Emily expressed their sympathy. She nodded, her face showing the strain.

"A great turnout. Quite a tribute to Edward," Nigel said, pumping her hand as if to congratulate her.

"I wasn't expecting this," Beryl said, withdrawing her hand and wiping it on her skirt. "I invited Edward's personal friends and some political colleagues, not this horde of strangers. The vicar is becoming alarmingly senile."

"We want to pay our respects to poor Edward," Vanessa said.

"How many of these people cared about Edward, do you suppose?" Beryl glared at Bridey Maguire and Rose Wilson, who were eagerly chatting as they came in the door and made a beeline for the buffet.

Emily could have assured her that Rose and Bridey had cared a great deal for Edward when he was a boy, but she didn't suppose it was a message Beryl wanted to hear.

"I imagine this lot will go home when we run out of food and drink. It won't be long."

"I'm so sorry for your loss," Nigel said, trying to bring their conversation to an appropriate end. "Edward was a good man, solid, dependable."

"Oh really. Is that what you think, Nigel?" Beryl's tone was surprisingly sharp.

"Of course."

Beryl turned away. The crowd enveloped Beryl, murmuring condolences.

"What was that about?" Emily whispered to Vanessa.

Vanessa shrugged. "She's probably loaded to the gills with antidepressants right now. Not making sense."

Emily noticed Clare Benson, wearing a purple dress and cloche trimmed with a black feather, sipping a glass of sherry. She was staring at Beryl. After making her excuses, Emily edged over to talk with her.

"I'm surprised to see you here," Emily said.

"I'm following the advice of counsel," Clare said. "My solicitor recommended that I attend the funeral as a childhood friend who was mourning Edward's passing would do."

"Not quite accurately," Emily said.

"It's a role I can play to perfection. Just watch."

Clare's eyes misted as she walked up to Beryl and put a hand on her sleeve. "Poor dear Edward. We shall not see his like again," she murmured.

"Have we met?" Beryl asked. She looked closely at Clare but apparently didn't recognize her from the screenshot in which she had been disguised.

"I'm Clare Benson. Edward and I were friends ever since we were children."

Beryl drew back. "Benson? Cyril's sister? Why did you come here?"

Without reacting, Clare continued. "I have such fond memories of Edward when he was a boy. We were best friends." She dabbed at her cheek with a lace handkerchief.

Beryl turned her back on Clare, her arms clenched around her body as if to keep herself from punching the woman.

Emily suspected Beryl would be even angrier if she had known that Clare was the woman who had impersonated her. Apparently, the police were keeping Sophie's accusation quiet while they investigated its authenticity.

To her surprise, Emily saw sorrow in Clare's eyes as she walked back to her. She wondered if Clare really was remembering their childhood friendship or if she was aware there might be an appreciative audience, including Emily, who would recall her reaction at the funeral.

"You were very convincing," Emily said.

"It wasn't all acting. When we were children, I loved Edward." Clare drew in a deep breath and made a hurried exit.

Emily looked over at the buffet table. A silver bowl of white Calla lilies and a variety of cheese snacks were spread on the lavender tablecloth, a Lenten color suitable for a funeral. She noticed a tall, elderly man with a great hooked nose and hooded eyes, lurking near the buffet. He was nibbling cheesy bits, their crumbs dropping onto his shirtfront. His eyes darted nervously around the room.

Emily overheard two women talking behind her.

"That's Henley, isn't it? The poor man looks ill at ease."

"As well he might. After the incident, I'm surprised he'd show his face here."

"Was he..."

"Oh yes. He was at Blanchley Hall at the time."

"Retired now, I suppose?"

"Early retirement. You can hardly be surprised that he didn't stay on after what happened."

Emily was curious. What had happened? Did it have anything to do with Edward's experience at Blanchley Hall? The secret he promised to keep? The housekeeper, Bridey Maguire, believed something dreadful had happened at school that created bad blood between Edward and Clare's brother Cyril. Emily wanted to hear more but the two women drifted away, munching on sausage rolls.

It wasn't hard for Emily to approach the man at the buffet for he stood alone despite the crowd. "Hello. Mr. Henley, isn't it? I heard you were one of Edward's favorite instructors at Blanchley Hall and I wanted to introduce myself. I'm Emily Swift, a friend of Vanessa and Nigel Chillingworth. I came here with them."

"Oh my, I see. Nigel's here too, is he? Well, well, I felt I must pay my respects to poor Edward's memory. Some people would think it inappropriate, but a prayer for the deceased and condolences to the bereaved are always right and proper, don't you think?"

"Definitely."

"Poor, poor boy."

"Was Edward happy at school? I heard there was some unfortunate occurrence."

The man drew back, his pale eyes widening. "I don't recall anything of the sort. I'm afraid I really must be going." His hand trembled as he put down his plate. He turned and stumped away, leaning on a cane.

Emily walked beside him. It wasn't hard to keep up. His speedy days were behind him. "I'm sorry. I didn't mean to upset you."

"Not at all. An important engagement. Must dash."

"Would you have time to talk to me later? I'm looking into the British school system. So different from ours in the United States. I have a friend whose boy might be going to Blanchley Hall next year and she's concerned about him."

"I'm hardly the right person to give advice. Please excuse me."

Emily was more curious than ever, but the old man was hurrying out the door, not even stopping to speak to Beryl.

Emily rejoined Vanessa, Jack and Nigel.

"Oh, there you are," Nigel said. "This crowd is getting to be a bit much. We've expressed our sympathy. Time to be going surely."

Emily wondered if there was more to be discovered. She noticed Jack was also gazing longingly toward the door. "Okay, let's say goodbye to our hostess," Emily said, leading the way to Beryl.

Beryl's wine glass was full, and her eyes were vague and unfocused.

"It's time for us to go," Vanessa said. "It was a lovely service."

"Edward will be sorely missed," Nigel said, bending close to Beryl. "I valued him as a friend and colleague."

"Did you indeed? Is that why you sent me those emails, maligning him?"

"Beg pardon?"

"You know what I mean."

Nigel looked baffled. "No, I never sent you emails. I wouldn't even know how to go about it. I don't have your email address."

Beryl sniffed, tossed her head and turned away.

"I swear I have no idea what the woman is talking about," Nigel said to Vanessa. He was clearly flustered.

Vanessa shrugged. "She appears to have been drinking a bit too much. And on top of the pills she was probably given..."

"Just a minute," Emily said. "I'll catch up with you outside." Emily followed Beryl into the pantry where she found her pouring herself a generous shot of Scotch.

"Sherry just isn't doing it for me today." Beryl held up her drink. "This has been a horrible day, and now everyone who ever heard of Edward is in my house, gawking. That senile old vicar has a lot to answer for. I wish these people would all clear out." She did not exclude Emily.

"Can we talk a minute? It's important." Emily didn't wait for an answer. She was pretty sure it would be "no." "Tell me about the emails you received. Nigel hardly knew Edward. Why would he malign him?"

"Hardly knew him? They were at school together. They have quite a history. Didn't Vanessa tell you? That's why Edward was blocking his advancement in the party. He knew him all too well."

Emily was stunned. Whatever happened at Blanchley Hall might have involved Nigel too.

"I can see that Vanessa didn't mention it. I wonder why since you're such great friends. Nigel loathed Edward. That's why he sent me the emails. I should have known Nigel was lying."

"What did he tell you?"

"He claimed that Edward was having an affair. Of course, I realized Nigel was trying to cause trouble, but I didn't think he'd make up such a story. He said Edward was going to meet his lover at the Inn."

Just as the maid suspected. "Is that why you went to the hotel? To confront him?"

"To catch him in the act. Yes. But I was the one who was fooled. When I looked in his room the first time, Edward was asleep, alone. Later, I found his body. It was horrible. I misjudged my husband and now he's dead. Why do you suppose Nigel lied to me?"

Her expression suggested she knew the answer.

Chapter 14

Outside Beryl Westley's cottage, the rain had stopped but gray clouds still loomed overhead. "Vanessa, I need to talk to you," Emily said.

"Of course. Come over to our place. We'll have a proper tea. All of us." Vanessa smiled at Jack.

"Can we meet alone? How about a walk?"

A shadow passed over Vanessa's face as she realized this would be a difficult conversation. "Fine."

"Let's follow the Cotswold Trail that leaves from town," Emily said.

"It will be wet and nasty. I have my pumps on, not exactly hiking boots."

Emily glanced down at her own feet. She had forgotten that she too was wearing shoes more suitable for a funeral than a tramp through soggy footpaths. "This afternoon then? Whenever and wherever you like."

Vanessa reluctantly agreed.

Emily and Jack said goodbye and headed back to the car. "We'll have to kill time until my walk with Vanessa," Emily said, taking his arm.

"No problem. Shall we go back to Badger's Hall? The snacks ran out pretty fast at Beryl's."

While enjoying the Savoury Platter, a sandwich on granary bread and a cup of tea, Emily told Jack what she had found out at the post-funeral gathering. "Beryl told me that Nigel was at Blanchley Hall in the same house as Edward and they had a 'quite a history,' as she put it. Apparently, they loathed each other."

"I thought Nigel hardly knew Edward."

"That's what he said, and Vanessa confirmed it, but Beryl told a different story."

"Very suspicious, if it's true."

"Beryl went to the hotel the night her husband died because an email from Nigel said Edward was meeting his lover there, but it wasn't true."

"It's odd she would be so quick to believe a message from Edward's enemy."

"Maybe Edward had transgressed in the past and Beryl assumed he was back to his old tricks and that Nigel enjoyed spreading the news and causing trouble. I stumbled across another clue. I noticed an elderly man grazing at the buffet and overheard some women commenting that he had been forced to leave Blanchley Hall after some unfortunate occurrence. When I asked him about it, he bolted."

"He must have been shocked to hear a total stranger ask about such a sensitive subject. Brits are not as forthcoming as we are."

"You think I overstepped?"

Jack laughed. "Of course, you did."

"I had to ask. Maybe the incident was one that involved Edward, Cyril and possibly Nigel. It could be important."

"So now Beryl thinks that Nigel lied to her because of a feud that started when those men were at prep school together?"

"Yes. The feud never ended. Edward was squelching Nigel's political ambitions. Beryl hinted that Nigel might be the killer and his lying email was meant to draw her to the inn and make her a suspect."

"Good lord."

"But Nigel denies sending *any* emails to Beryl. He looked completely baffled."

"So he did. But perhaps he's a good liar."

"I don't believe Nigel sent those emails. Why would he? Because of an incident that occurred years ago when he was a boy? It doesn't seem plausible."

Jack took both her hands. His blue eyes softened with concern. "Dear heart, like a true friend, you're trying to help Vanessa. It would be an ugly, ironic twist if saving Sophie would mean implicating Vanessa's husband in a murder. Maybe this is a good time to back away and let the authorities deal with this case."

"Oh, Jack, I do hope Vanessa isn't married to a killer. If she is, it's all the more reason that I have to find out about it. But I don't think Nigel's guilty. He seems like such a kind, harmless fellow."

"We don't know him," Jack reminded her.

"Beryl was awfully eager to throw him under the bus. She may have a strong motive to do so."

"She's your prime suspect?"

"Definitely."

Later that afternoon, Vanessa met Emily in Stratford and they walked along the River Avon, following the walkway in front of the Royal Shakespeare Company, commonly called the RSC. Emily paused to admire the swans drifting majestically in the green water and wondered if they were descendants of those in Shakespeare's time. She drew a deep breath and plunged into the topic troubling her mind. "Vanessa, I know you don't want to talk to me about your husband and I understand that, but if Beryl is trying to frame him or implicate him in the murder, we have to get at the truth."

Vanessa looked shocked. "What do you mean? Why would she do that?"

Emily told her about her conversation in the pantry. "Beryl said Nigel had 'quite a history' with Edward. I think she suspects Nigel killed him. Or she's pretending she does. Why did you tell me Nigel barely knew Edward?"

"It's basically the truth. They haven't met socially since they were at Blanchley Hall together. That was donkeys' years ago. I didn't tell you Nigel was at school with Edward because it would have been misleading. You would have wondered if he could be a suspect. Nigel isn't capable of murder. I know him."

The words reminded Emily of those Vanessa had said to her years ago, warming her heart. Of course, she would be even more fiercely loyal to her husband than she was to Emily. But was she right about Nigel? Blind loyalty has its pitfalls.

"I asked Nigel again about the emails," Vanessa said. "He insisted that he never sent them. I believe him. Why would he?"

"I heard there was an incident at Blanchley Hall involving Nigel, Edward and Cyril that caused a rift among the boys," Emily said, exaggerating her knowledge quite a bit. "Do you know about it?"

"No. Going away to school was hard for Nigel. He was close to his family and the separation was painful. I'm afraid there was bullying at school. Nigel has bad memories, but he doesn't want to talk about them. It's almost like PTSD. Sometimes he has nightmares and thinks he's back at school."

"Good lord. Didn't you ask him why?"

"Of course, I did. Nigel said there were just some silly pranks. I didn't ask again. Bringing up the subject made him miserable. I trust him. I don't need to know every detail of his life."

Emily did not feel so restrained. She couldn't wait to do her research.

Back in her room at the Adelphi House, Emily burst in on Jack.

"Did Vanessa tell all?" he asked, looking up from his computer.

"Not exactly. But I do have a lead."

Emily pulled out her computer and typed in "Pranks at Blanchley Hall." The result was immediate. She quickly scanned the article, published twenty years ago, then read aloud to Jack with increasing horror.

Boys' Game Proves Fatal

Suspicions of foul play or suicide at one of the nation's most prestigious schools were put to rest today when the Coroner reached the verdict of "misadventure" in the death of Arthur Farraday, a 15-year-old student at Blanchley Hall.

An inquest heard that the boy had been playing a game during which he was strangled with his dressing gown cord.

One of the boys gave this account of how the game was played. "We sit on a chair and a cord is wrapped around our neck. One of our friends pulls the ends of the cord until we faint. It's only supposed to last a few minutes." This time it ended in tragedy.

Housemaster Neal Henley of Smedley House said he was shocked that such intelligent boys would do something so foolish. "We can't watch these boys every minute. If they are determined to outwit us, they will."

The boys who played the game refused to reveal who was pulling the cord when Farraday died. Now that the Coroner has ruled the death a "misadventure," it is unlikely that efforts to determine the boy's identity will continue.

"All the students who played the game are equally at fault in this tragic accident," said Housemaster Henley. "I have told them very clearly that the fainting game must never be played again."

"That's horrible," Emily said. "It's certainly more than a boyhood prank. If Edward was no longer going to keep the boy's identity a secret, it could be a motive for murder."

"Especially if political aspirations are involved," Jack said. "It could end a career. Do you suppose Edward was blackmailing someone?"

"It's possible. I have to talk to Housemaster Henley."

The mystery of who killed Edward had acquired a new urgency for Emily. If her friend was married to a killer, Emily had to expose him even if it meant the end of their friendship. And if Nigel was innocent—which she believed—Emily had to make sure he wasn't falsely accused. Beryl could easily end his career by making insinuations, smearing his name. Mud sticks even if the victim is later exonerated.

Emily found Henley's address online and drove to his home the next day. He lived in a small stone cottage in a row of identical homes in Bourton on the Water. Emily found the ex-schoolmaster trimming a bay hedge in his tiny front garden. A border collie was sitting beside him, apparently supervising the work.

"Remember me?" Emily called out as she stepped out of the car. "We met after Edward Westley's funeral."

"Ah, yes. Certainly. Good day." Henley raised his canvas garden hat as if it were a top hat. "I've just finished here. Chores to do inside. Must dash." He dropped his clippers on the ground, leaving the pile of brush and stumped toward the door, limping heavily but without his stick this time. His dog was right at his heels.

Emily followed him. The dog faced her and started barking, leaning down on its front paws. "Good doggie. Nice doggie." Its tail was not wagging.

"Quiet, Flora," Henley ordered, and the dog fell silent, leaning against him, still looking at Emily as if daring her to take a step closer. "She's quite protective. A loyal shepherd."

"I see that."

"If you give her a treat, she'll like you better." Henley reached into his pocket and pulled out a couple of biscuits and handed them to Emily.

She tossed one to the dog who caught it in one gulp and put the other in the pocket of her skirt. "I brought you some lemon curd and strawberry jam as a peace offering," Emily said. "I know I was rude to you the other day, but I did have a good reason. I'm helping the police with their inquiries into Edward's murder."

"Not assisting a friend whose boy wants to go to Blanchley Hall?"

Drat. Unlike Emily, Henley had not forgotten her lame excuse for accosting him at the funeral. "Well, that too, of course, but, most importantly, helping the police. Whatever happened years ago at Blanchley House could help us find out who killed him."

"No, certainly not. Too long ago."

"I suspect an innocent person may be charged or at least come under suspicion. I want to prevent that if I can. When I looked for a common factor among the people who might have killed Westley, I realized they had been at Blanchley Hall together years ago. Do you remember the fainting game?"

Henley looked as if he might faint himself. He looked around the small plot of grass in front of his house as if it could contain an escape route hitherto undiscovered. "You're very persistent, Miss...."

"Swift. Emily Swift. Here, do accept my peace offerings." She thrust the jars of jam into his unwilling hands.

Henley sighed. "Well then, I suppose if it's a police matter. Come on inside."

Emily felt a pang of guilt at misrepresenting her role once again. The lies were piling up. "It's a matter of justice anyway," she clarified.

"I'm afraid there's not much in the larder," Henley said as he led the way into his parlor. "The lad who brings my groceries is coming later today. I'm even out of tea. So, I can't offer you anything. I suppose you'll just be a few minutes anyway," Henley added hopefully.

Flora circled three times and curled up in a dog bed in front of the brick fireplace. School trophies marched in a line across the wooden mantel. Untidy stacks of books were piled atop the full bookcases lining the walls. Henley sank into an armchair, apparently his usual seat judging by the deep indentation in its cushion. "What do you want to know?"

"Who was involved in the fainting game?"

"I certainly can't tell you that. It was a police matter. They would know. So, if you really are working with the police you have access to that information."

"Juvenile records are sealed."

"Quite properly in my opinion. How did you find out about it?" Henley asked. "It happened so long ago."

"News lives forever on the internet."

"God help us. This modern age is beyond me."

"Did Cyril Benson play the fainting game? Since he passed away years ago, it can't hurt to tell me."

Henley sighed. "Cyril was a challenging boy. He resisted discipline. And he exerted quite a hold on boys who weren't as self-confident and aggressive. He didn't always use his influence for the best. Still his death was tragic. Especially so soon after the...the other matter...the game, if you will."

"So, the answer is yes? Cyril was involved?"

"I can't be more specific. If you read the news article, you know as much as we felt should be released to the public. The boys were so young."

"But now they're grown men. Two of them died in suspicious circumstances."

Henley looked shocked. "Edward, yes. Terribly shocking. But Cyril's death was an automobile accident. Surely there's no connection. I don't know why you've fixed on an incident that happened years ago as key to the murder."

Seeing his agitation, Emily changed the topic. "You're no longer at Blanchley Hall?"

"No. I didn't feel I could stay on. The headmaster was kind enough to say I wouldn't be removed from my post, but parents were complaining and threatening to take their boys out. Something had to be done to restore confidence in the school. My very early retirement took care of a knotty problem."

"Was it your idea? To resign?"

"Oh, well. Up to a point. The possibility was suggested to me, of course."

"Were the boys who played the game punished?"

"No. It was felt that the death of their friend was punishment enough. The sooner the incident was forgotten, the better. Especially for the reputation of the school."

Emily wondered if Henley could be seeking revenge after all these years. He had sounded resentful of the boys in the newspaper interview. "Do you blame the boys for ending your career?" Emily asked bluntly.

"I suppose I did at the time. They were supposed to be the cream of the crop, the brightest boys in England, destined for top leadership positions, and they acted like idiots following the lead of one charismatic boy. But now, no. Time has passed. They're adults. I moved on years ago. I have my garden, my books."

"Was Nigel Chillingworth a friend of Cyril's?"

"All the boys in Smedley House were friends to some extent. There are only fifty boys in each of the houses at Blanchley Hall."

"So, you must have known all the boys in Smedley very well. What was your impression of Nigel? Was he a bully like Cyril?"

"Oh, no. I doubt that he took any pleasure in tormenting boys weaker than himself. He wasn't that sort of boy, not at heart. I asked him outright why he joined Cyril in ridiculing anyone who was different, not good at games, a bit overweight. One poor lad, who stuttered, was teased until he broke down and cried. He had to leave school. When the taxi came to take him away, Cyril, Nigel and a few other boys stood outside as he left, yelling, "GGGGood-bbbye," and laughing. After that I talked to Nigel. 'You can't think that was funny, or kind? Why did you do it?' He told me he was afraid not to be part of Cyril's inner circle. If you weren't with him, you were an outsider and could easily become a victim. He was afraid of Cyril. Fascinated by him too, I think."

"What about the boy who died? Farraday? Was he a victim?"

"Oh, yes. Poor boy. He wanted to be seen as one of the lads. Not a weakling." Henley wiped away a bead of sweat that was trickling down the side of his cheek. "Would you care for a cup of tea?" he asked, apparently forgetting that he had claimed to be out of tea.

"No, thank you."

"Well, if you don't mind, I'll just get myself one. I'm feeling a bit parched. I'll bring you a cup just in case." He had trouble launching himself from the deep chair, pushing off with both hands. He grabbed his cane and hobbled into the kitchen.

As soon as he was out of the room, Emily walked over to look more closely at the many photos that lined the walls. In each one, schoolboys in black robes with high white collars, stood on the steps of a brick, ivy covered building presumably Smedley House. She looked for Nigel but if he was there, she didn't recognize him. Along with the photos hung two framed documents with Latin inscriptions in florid calligraphy: *Per unitatem vis* and *Pro domo sua.*

"You recall your Latin, of course," Henley said coming back with two cups of tea wobbling in his hands.

"Sadly no. I only took two years. *Unitatem* must be something about unity?" Emily took a cup and thanked him.

"Correct. "Through unity strength," and "For one's house". These mottos hung in Smedley to remind the boys of the importance of loyalty to their house and school."

"You taught Latin then?"

"Indeed, I did. It was out of vogue for some years, but our school does not follow the shifting tides of public opinion. We stick to a classic curriculum. I am pleased to say that more boys choose Latin every year. It should, of course, be required not an option." He sniffed.

Emily complimented him on the tea, which she found surprisingly delicious, clearly not the result of a hastily dipped tea bag, then she returned to the subject Henley must have hoped she had abandoned. "I wonder about Farraday's parents. Do you know where they are now?"

"Oh yes, I go down to Avebury where they live and place a few flowers on Arthur's grave from time to time. They're lovely people. Not a word of reproach to me."

"Were they at the funeral?" Emily asked.

"I don't believe so, no." Henley took a deep drink of tea, then placed it on a side table. He leaned his head back and closed his eyes as if preparing to take a nap.

Emily cleared her throat.

His eyelids fluttered open. "Sorry. Feeling a bit knackered. I suppose you'll have to be going soon."

Emily realized she wouldn't be able to drag any more information out of him. He didn't have the narrative talent of Bridey or Rose. Too bad those chatty women didn't know the inside scoop.

"You've been very kind, Mr. Henley. I know this hasn't been easy for you."

Back at the Adelphi House, Emily found Jack in their room lying on the bed, his laptop on his knees, staring at the screen. "Are you working on your article?" She enjoyed turning the tables on him. Jack did not have a monopoly on this particular query. She knew he had more work to do on his clinical article on the effects of childhood trauma on health in adulthood.

"No, in fact, I'm looking for information on treating anorexia nervosa."

"For Brendan?"

"Exactly." Jack closed his laptop. "I'm not finding anything new. What about you? Is Henley a likely suspect? A man intent on getting revenge for his ruined career?"

"He does have a motive. It must have been hard on him to be forced into early retirement. His home is filled with memorabilia of his years at Blanchley Hall, photos of the boys and their game-day trophies. Nothing to indicate other interests except a very small garden. His life seems to have come to an abrupt end twenty years ago."

"A suspect then?"

"He didn't seem to have sufficient strength or energy to launch a killing spree. He's quite old and a bit lame."

"Too bad. He would have been a convenient suspect."

"I know."

Chapter 15

"Don't do anything risky while I'm gone," Jack advised Emily the next morning. He was taking the train up to London to meet a colleague who was in the UK to attend a medical conference on the impact of trauma on the health of immigrant children and teens. "I'll have lunch with Glen, hear about his conference and be back here tonight. You'll probably want to work on your article," Jack said.

Emily wrinkled her nose at him. "Oh, I will." In fact, she had been busy writing about the delights of Stratford upon Avon and was almost ready to fire her article off to George. Her editor did seem a bit impatient.

"Good. No time to track down a dangerous killer then." Jack kissed her and hurried out the door.

As soon as she was alone, Emily called Vanessa. "Can we meet? I have something to tell you."

"Not today, sorry. I have a hairdresser appointment in London. Travis is the only one who can cope with my unruly mop."

In fact, Emily had always envied Vanessa's perfectly groomed hair, so unlike her own, which burst into wild curls at the first hint of humidity. "How about tomorrow then? I've made some interesting discoveries."

"Of course. I'm in the car now, can't talk. I'll ring you."

Hmm. Vanessa was becoming evasive. Maybe she knew more about her husband's relationship with Edward than she was willing to admit.

Emily decided to seize this opportunity to talk to Nigel alone without Vanessa running interference. She drove over to Chillingworth Manor and parked in the roundabout. When she rang the bell, a middle-aged woman in a maid's black uniform opened the door a crack.

"Sorry, ma'am. The Manor isn't open to visitors and school groups today."

"I'm here to see Nigel."

"Is he expecting you?" Her tone was perfectly cordial, but she didn't invite Emily inside.

"Not exactly."

"I thought not. He's working on one of his projects today and wouldn't like to be disturbed. Not when he's making one of his 'improvements' to the grounds." She sounded as if she heartily disapproved of whatever he might be up to.

"You might just tell him I'm here," Emily suggested.

"If he were in the house, of course, I would have done that straight away. But he's not. He's somewhere on the grounds."

"Well, then I might just have a look round."

"I wouldn't do that, ma'am. The dog." The woman shut the door.

Emily walked around the side of the house to the maze and formal flower garden and gazed down at the green field where the falconry and stable stood. She scanned the area for Nigel but didn't see him. Then she heard hoarse barking. The lurcher came bounding up the hill toward her.

"Nigel!" she called out. He was beyond the sound of her voice, but she could see him bent over a worktable in front of the stable. What was the damn dog's name?

Digger, she recalled just as he slid to a stop in front of her.

Emily reached into her pocket for the last of the biscuits Henley had given her. Luckily, she was once more wearing her khaki travel skirt with its many pockets. "Hey, Digger, good boy, good doggie." She tossed the biscuit in the air and he caught it in one gulp, then sat and looked at her expectantly.

"Sorry, all out of treats," she said, spreading her hands.

Nigel was hurrying up the hill. "It's okay, Digger. She's a friend. What a surprise," he said turning to Emily. He was wearing corduroy trousers, a loose gray sweater and work boots. "Vanessa's not at home. She'll be sorry to have missed you."

"Your assistant said you were working on a project." Emily looked at him with keen interest, hoping to put him in a receptive mood.

"Yes. Quite exciting actually. I'm going to set up a haunted experience—ghosts, scary sounds, that sort of thing. I've been researching sound systems, considering where to put speakers." His blue eyes gleamed with excitement.

"You've really embraced Vanessa's plans to make Chillingworth a paying proposition."

"Yes, I have. Not everyone approves. Vanessa hasn't really been welcomed into the community. Not her fault. She's blamed for not keeping Chillingworth exactly as it always has been. People don't realize the alternative would be to give it away or let it fall into ruin."

"So nobody criticizes *you* for the changes?"

"Oddly enough, no. Our neighbors think Vanessa forced her plans on me."

"I expect you're quick to set them straight," Emily said.

"Naturally," Nigel said, looking back at his worktable by the stable. "I'll tell Vanessa you popped in."

"Yes, do. Just a quick question before I let you get back to work."

"Of course."

"I ran into Mr. Henley at the funeral. Your old housemaster. Did you have a chance to talk with him?"

Nigel turned pale and backed away from her. "No, I didn't see him. It's been years. Probably wouldn't have recognized him anyway."

"I learned about the fainting game." Emily let him think Henley was her source. "It must have been a dreadful experience for you boys."

"I had nothing whatever to do with it. Of course, I knew what happened. It was a great scandal at the time. It was in all the newspapers. Mater was shocked. She almost pulled me out of school. But it had nothing to do with me."

"I understand Cyril was the ringleader. You were friends, weren't you?"

"Friends? Not as I would use the word. I knew him, of course. Smedley House was small. Cyril was a leader. It was important to keep in his good graces."

"What would happen if you didn't?"

Nigel looked puzzled.

"Keep in his good graces."

"What do you mean? Nothing." Nigel was becoming more and more agitated. In sympathy, the lurcher was making rapid circles around his legs, whining.

"But you did play the game?"

"Me? No, of course not. Why are you raking this up now? It was years ago."

"You know Vanessa wants me to find out who killed Edward because she's afraid her friend Sophie will be falsely convicted."

"This has nothing to do with Edward's unfortunate death."

"Doesn't it? Two of the boys who were involved in the game have died under suspicious circumstances. Cyril and Edward."

"Nonsense. Cyril died ages ago, the year we left Blanchley Hall. It was an accident. No connection."

"If someone is seeking revenge at this late date, you could be in danger, Nigel." *Or guilty*, Emily thought.

Nigel knotted his hands into fists and glared at her. "I told you I never played that goddamn game. There would be no reason for anyone to come after me."

Emily heard Vanessa's voice yelling, "Halloo!" She hurried toward them, then stopped when she saw Nigel's face, which had deepened to purple. A vein in his temple was throbbing.

"Oh, my dear. What's the matter?" Vanessa wheeled on Emily. "What have you said to him?" She sounded like a lioness pouncing to protect her young.

"Shall I tell her?" Emily asked Nigel quietly.

"You've said enough." He turned and walked rapidly down the hill.

"He looks so upset, poor lamb. What happened? Did you tell him that Beryl is trying to cast suspicion on him?"

"I didn't get that far," Emily said. "Do you really want to know what we were talking about?"

"Of course."

"Your hair looks very nice, by the way." It looked exactly the same.

"Thank you. So?"

Emily told her friend what she had found out about the fainting game.

"And you think Nigel was involved in this 'game'?" There was a sharp edge to Vanessa's voice.

"I don't know. He says he wasn't."

"Well, there you are then. Nigel never lies."

Chapter 16

As Vanessa walked Emily to her car, she avoided looking at her, while still pretending that nothing was wrong. "I wish my parents had lived to see Chillingworth Manor," Vanessa said, embarking on a safe subject. "How they would have loved it!"

"Yes," Emily agreed. "They would have been proud of what you've done to preserve this slice of British history." Emily thought of Vanessa's mother and her love of everything British. As she said goodbye, Emily reached out to hug her friend as she usually did.

Vanessa drew away. "Sorry, a bit of a cold. I don't want you to catch it."

"Oh, Vanessa, don't be angry with me. I'm just doing what you asked me to do."

"I didn't ask you to make crazy accusations against my husband."

"I'm not accusing him, I'm investigating."

"You don't trust my judgment," Vanessa snapped, giving up the pretense that all was well between them. "Don't you think I'd know if Nigel were the kind of man who would play such a vicious game and then lie about it? Someone who would kill to keep it secret?"

"I don't think he's guilty. Really. I was just trying to consider every possibility."

"You should have a little faith in me. I'm not a complete idiot. I know my husband." Unappeased, Vanessa turned away and stalked back to the manor.

On the drive back to the Adelphi House, Emily thought about her long friendship with Vanessa going back to the time when she was Vivian. Her home had been a haven for Emily when she was a child. Emily recalled one evening—one of many—when her parents were yelling at each other. She was lying in bed, the covers pulled up over her head, trying not to listen. She looked over at her older sister Fanny sprawled out in bed like a starfish. She was sound asleep. Then Emily heard smashing, breaking glass, a scream, then a loud yell. She was terrified. Maybe one of her parents was going to kill the other? She wished Fanny would wake up and comfort her, but her sister didn't stir.

Emily got out of bed, dressed quickly, threw her Barbie and PJs in her pink backpack and ran down the stairs and out the back door. She walked through the dark starless night to Vanessa's house a block away and rang the bell.

"Emily, how nice to see you," Vivian's mother said, as if this were a social call. She didn't mention Emily's tear-stained face or ask why she was shivering. Emily hadn't wanted to go to the front hall to get her coat.

"Would you like to stay here tonight? Vivian would love to have you."

Emily looked up the stairs and saw her friend's eager face, peering over the bannister. "Yes, do stay!" she called out. "Did you bring your Barbies?" she asked, bounding down the stairs.

She stopped when she saw Emily's red, teary eyes. "What's wrong?"

Her mother took Vivian's arm and looked into her eyes. "No personal questions, dear. It's not polite."

Emily was grateful to be out of the battlefield. In Vivian's quiet, peaceful home, it didn't seem likely that murder and mayhem could be going on at her own.

"I'll just call your mum to let her know, shall I?"

Emily nodded.

When Mrs. Kent came back to say that it was perfectly fine to stay, Emily felt a flood of relief. She took it as a good sign that Mrs. Kent hadn't mentioned that one of Emily's parents had killed the other. Surely that would have come up in their phone conversation if it had happened.

Emily and Vivian stayed up late, playing "Barbie dolls go to a royal wedding." Mrs. Kent didn't come in to insist they turn out the lights until it was ten o'clock.

Emily had many dear friends, but no one shared her history the way Vanessa did. She saw the cruel irony of her situation. Emily had become involved in the murder investigation as a favor to Vanessa and now it was causing a rift between them. But Emily had to find out who had killed Edward. It was for Vanessa's own good. If Nigel was a murderer, Vanessa had to know. He seemed harmless, but then, as Jack kept reminding her, she didn't really know him. She wanted to trust Vanessa's judgment, but she suspected her friend might be too kind, too trusting. Her peaceful childhood had led her to believe the world was a safe place. Emily had no such illusions. If someone was trying to kill the boys who had been involved in the fainting game, Nigel had to be alerted to the danger.

Emily knew from past experience that finding out all she could about the victim would be helpful. She resolved to talk to Clare, the actor who had impersonated Beryl and hired Sophie to terrify Edward with snakes.

Emily waited for Clare on the banks of the Avon where the wind was blowing over the water sending swans reeling. When Clare came out of the theatre, wearing a crimson cloak with its hood thrown back to reveal her jet-black hair, she stopped and glared at Emily. "You again. What are you doing here?"

"Watching the poor swans struggle in the wind while I wait for you."

Clare glanced at the swans. "'I have seen a swan with bootless labour swim against the tide and spend her strength with over-matching waves,'" she quoted.

"The Bard seems to have a quote for every occasion," Emily said. "As an actor, you have them on the tip of your tongue. I envy that." Emily smiled in what she hoped was a winsome, admiring way.

"I'm not going to answer any more of your questions. We open in a week and I've just had a very long, tiring rehearsal."

"Oh, dear. You need a glass of wine," Emily said. She hoped her voice oozed sympathy. "My treat. The Garrick again?"

Clare sighed. "You don't give up, do you?"

Seated in the cozy niche at the back of the ancient pub, Emily sipped her lager. "I found out about the fainting game."

"So?" There was a flicker of alarm in Clare's eyes.

"Tell me about it."

"Why on earth are you interested?" Clare sipped her wine. "Ancient history."

"Because it could help us find out who killed Edward. You must want the real killer found. You're in an awkward position, aren't you? Sophie must have told the police about you by now."

"They interviewed me this morning." Clare's voice was flat. She looked away.

"Were they satisfied with your answers?"

Clare sighed. "They said I would hear from them again and advised me not to leave town."

"It would be a shame if they held you for questioning just as your play is about to open. You're probably a person of interest."

Clare glared at her. "I can't imagine how you can help. But fine. What do you want to know?"

"I suspect the fainting game caused the hostility between Edward and Cyril. Why? What happened?"

"I might as well tell you." Clare paused and focused her dark eyes above Emily's head as if seeing the past unfold on the wooden wainscoting. She drew in a deep dramatic breath and lowered her voice. "When the boys came home on holiday, right after the tragedy, Edward told me that Cyril had started the fainting game at school. The boys had discovered the pleasures of oxygen deprivation quite by accident. Cyril tackled a boy on the playing field, and he fainted. When he came to, the boy was giggling. He liked the tingly, dizzy feeling, a high like spinning around in a circle until you fall down. It was Cyril's idea that they induce this feeling on purpose. Somehow, they discovered a way to do it. Edward told me he never played the game himself and tried to stop the other boys. He told them it was dangerous, but Cyril just laughed at him."

"What happened the day Farraday died?"

"Edward claimed that Cyril forced one of the boys to pull the cord around his neck and keep tightening it until Farraday collapsed. Then Cyril said, 'He's faking,' and grabbed the cord himself and continued to pull."

"So, Cyril killed him?"

"No, no. That's what Edward told me, but it wasn't true. When I heard Edward's story, I was horrified. But my brother swore to me that Edward was lying. I believed him. All the boys were in it together, Cyril said. It was just a bit of fun, rough housing the way boys do, an accident. It was just Farraday's bad luck that it went on too long. Cyril denied grabbing the cord.

"Edward told me he thought it was his duty to tell Henley exactly what had happened, or rather his version of it, including Cyril's role. He had kept mum when the headmaster and Farraday's parents asked him what happened because he was afraid of what Cyril would do if he spoke up. But as time went on he felt more and more guilty about keeping the secret.

"Cyril was sure everything would be fine if Edward just kept his mouth shut. All the other boys were sticking together, he told me. As long as no one boy was accused, it would be okay. I understood. After all, it was an accident. Nobody meant to hurt Farraday.

"But Edward couldn't see that. He was tormented with guilt. Finally, he told me he had decided to tell his headmaster when he went back to school."

"But he didn't. Why did he decide to keep quiet?"

"I begged him. He promised me he'd keep the secret. We were very close then. That's why he confided in me in the first place. He expected me to believe him instead of my brother. How could I do that?"

"So, Edward gave you his word. Everything was going to be fine, or so you thought. But then your brother died in a car accident. Why did you suspect Edward ran over him on purpose?"

"I didn't suspect. I knew."

"Why would he do that?"

"He was ashamed of what he'd done, and he blamed Cyril."

"Ashamed? But Edward didn't play the game."

"So he said. Cyril claimed that he did, and I believe my brother. I think the guilt preyed on Edward's mind and the only way he could find relief was to kill Cyril."

"You don't have any doubts? No possibility that it might have been an accident?"

"No. I knew how much Edward hated Cyril. And he was afraid of him. Edward was not a brave lad. When I saw that car speed up and saw the look on his face, I knew."

"Wow. If Edward was that vindictive, he must have made a lot of enemies. Do you have any idea who had a motive to kill him?" Aside from yourself, Emily thought.

"I don't know. It probably has nothing to do with what happened at Blanchley Hall. That was so long ago."

"I'm curious about the other boys who were involved. What about Nigel Chillingworth? Did he play the game?"

"He must have. He was a great admirer of my brother. Came to our house all the time."

Emily's heart sank. If Edward had been planning to reveal the names of the boys who played the game, it could have destroyed Nigel's career. A powerful motive for murder. Vanessa would be devastated if Nigel was guilty.

Chapter 17

When Jack returned from London that evening, Emily hurried to hug him. He folded her in his arms and pulled her close.

"How was your lunch with Glen?" Emily asked.

"Interesting. He was enthusiastic about the conference and I wanted to hear all about it. As you know, the effect of trauma is close to the subject of my own article."

Jack stroked her back. "You feel tense. What is it? Is something wrong?"

Emily drew back. She didn't want to change the subject quite so quickly, but she couldn't help rushing to confide in Jack. "I did find out something troubling. Clare told me that Nigel was much closer to her brother Cyril than he led us to believe. In fact, he was a frequent visitor to their house. She says he must have played the fainting game—even though he denies it. If true, this could have given him a motive for murder."

"So, you think Edward might have been going to name names at this late date? Why would he?"

"I don't know. But it's possible. I don't want to believe it. Vanessa is furious with me for even considering Nigel a suspect."

"I think you're focusing on the worst possible scenario."

Emily took a deep breath. "You're right. There are other more likely suspects. For instance, Beryl. She was at the Inn the night Edward died and she could have planted the poison. She was quick to believe her husband was being unfaithful. Maybe she already suspected. She could have been planning to poison him in any case and the snakes were just a coincidence."

"It's possible."

"I want to talk to her, get her perspective on the fainting game. Edward may have told her his version of what happened at school. Maybe she knows what he was planning to do next."

"I'll go with you."

The next morning, Jack and Emily parked in front of Beryl Westley's picture-perfect cottage where a groundsman, whose tan, weather-beaten face attested to a life of outdoor labor, was trimming a topiary shaped like a lollypop near the doorway. Emily commented on the sunniness of the day.

"Won't last," he rasped without looking at her. "Rain before noon."

Emily glanced at the cloudless sky and shrugged. Seeing no bell to press, she clanged the lion's-head doorknocker.

"You won't find Mrs. Westley to home."

"How disappointing. I don't suppose you know where she is?"

"Course I do. Where she is most days. At her real estate office in town."

Emily had thought of Beryl only in her role as the victim's wife. It hadn't occurred to her to wonder what else she did but, of course, Beryl must have a career or do volunteer work. "Thanks. I'll go to her office."

The gardener sniffed. "Won't do you much good to track her down if you're planning a bit of a chat. When Mrs. Westley's at work, she only talks to folks as are looking for properties. Expensive properties."

Well, why not? Emily would enjoy looking at expensive properties.

Emily and Jack drove to the center of Chipping Campden and parked in front of the Westley real estate office, a small stone building with a bay window that displayed a poster with photos of lavish homes. Emily aimed her phone at the most expensive house and snapped a photo.

Inside, a receptionist was typing rapidly, her eyes fixed on her computer screen. Emily asked to speak to Mrs. Westley.

"Do you have an appointment?" The young woman's eyes flicked from her screen to Emily.

"Unfortunately, no. But my husband and I are in town for such a short time. I was hoping she could fit us in."

Jack looked startled.

"I'll check." The young woman stood up and headed toward the back of the office.

"Husband?" Jack whispered. "I don't remember our wedding. Did I enjoy it?"

"Shh. Married couples are the ones who buy houses."

Before the receptionist had a chance to summon her, Beryl strode through the row of desks that filled the small office and fixed Emily with a steely eye. "What are you doing here?"

"Jack and I have fallen in love with the Cotswolds. We'd like to see some of the homes you have for sale."

"Oh please. You're not planning to move to England."

"No, of course not. But my mother is quite the anglophile and she might buy a property here to enjoy during her retirement. She watches British shows on TV all the time. She's a fan of Penelope Keith, the woman who goes driving through the British countryside from one charming village to another. Mom never misses an episode."

Beryl looked skeptical. "Your mother? Is she here then?"

"No, but I could do some advance work for her."

"This is quite a posh area. Are you sure it's the right place for your mum?" Beryl shot an unflattering glance at Emily's travel outfit: a black skirt with many pockets, beige camp shirt and sandals.

"My mother's very well off," Emily lied. "Price would be no object." Emily, a fan of the annual Parade of Homes, always went straight to see mega mansions on Lake Minnetonka that she could never possibly afford. So much fun to look. She hoped Jack was not snickering. She didn't dare look at him.

"There's not much available right now. Perhaps if your mother came to England..."

"I saw a photo in the window of a house I think would be perfect for her. We could take a look and I'll send her photos." Emily held up her phone helpfully, showing a screen shot of an ad for a huge stone house with a sunroom and patio. A tall hedge enclosed its vast lawn. The price was listed at 900,000 pounds.

Beryl sighed. She clearly didn't believe Emily but, surrounded as she was by her office staff, could not easily refuse and thus set a poor example by dismissing potential customers. "Cheltenham, is it? A bit of a drive."

"Not too far for us," Jack said. "My cousin and I made it in half an hour the other day."

"Hmm. You're lucky you weren't ticketed. I'd estimate closer to an hour." She turned to one of her staff and asked her to cover her afternoon appointments. "All right. Let's get on with it."

Beryl led them to a deep burgundy vintage car parked by the door. "It's easiest if we travel in the same car, don't you think?"

"Wow," Jack, ran his hand over the car, stroking it as if it were a beloved horse. "A vintage Morris. What year is it?"

"It's a 1947 Morris Eight series. It was Edward's pride and joy." Beryl opened the back door. "He never let me drive it." Jack climbed in, but Emily settled herself beside Beryl in the front.

"Don't you two want to sit together?" Beryl asked. "Feel free to move, Emily."

An odd suggestion, Emily thought, as if Beryl were their chauffeur. She probably wanted to avoid the questions Emily intended to ask her. "I might get carsick in the back." Emily was afraid her fingers would be permanently crossed after all her fibs. She turned to look at Jack. "You don't mind, do you?" He would easily guess why she wanted to be close to Beryl.

"No, I can spread out back here. Lots of leg room."

Beryl turned on BBC radio and bumped up the volume.

"Do you mind?" Jack said. "I'm sensitive to noise."

"Aren't you the delicate couple? How nice you've found one another." Beryl switched off the radio.

Emily had wisely chosen to view a house that was more than a half hour away. She leaned back in the soft leather seat and relaxed as she enjoyed the drive. Chattering happily, she commented on the beautiful countryside and recounted highlights of her trip, then at last she introduced the topic that was uppermost in her mind. "The last time we met, I thought you sounded a little suspicious of Nigel. I couldn't imagine why. Now I get it." She hoped this comment would be enigmatic enough to pique Beryl's interest.

Beryl sighed. "I thought that was your real reason for this expedition. Should I turn around right now?"

"No. I'm serious about wanting to see the house. My mother really is considering moving to England for her retirement." (At least her mother had once said, "Oh how lovely to live there!" when Penelope had pointed out a particularly quaint village.)

"Right."

"But we can multitask. I've talked to Headmaster Henley as well as to Clare and Nigel. I found out about the fainting game."

The car swerved and Beryl wrenched the wheel, setting the car back in the correct lane. "Why in hell? Who do you think you are? A reincarnation of Miss Marple?"

"I think what happened in the fainting game is the reason Edward was killed. If your husband confided in you, the version he told you is likely to be the most accurate. But maybe he didn't tell you."

"Of course, he did," Beryl snapped. "Edward told me everything. That damned game. It scarred him for life. He had nightmares that woke him up screaming, thinking he was back in school. The boy who died, Arthur Farraday, was his closest friend. Edward never played the fainting game. He thought it was dangerous. But Cyril liked it. He liked it a lot. Sometimes he played it alone in his room. You know what I mean. Autoerotic pleasures. And he insisted the other boys play. Edward was there the night Arthur died. He saw it all.

"Cyril was a bully. Poor Arthur didn't dare refuse him. He'd be called a wimp if he didn't play. Some boys just pretended to faint so the game would stop. That's what Cyril thought Arthur was doing when he slumped over. Faking. And maybe he was. That's why Cyril grabbed the cord when the other boy dropped it and kept on pulling. He was the one who was finally responsible."

"If Edward and Arthur were such good friends, no wonder Edward was furious at Cyril. Clare thinks that's why he drove his car right into her brother and killed him."

"Ridiculous. Edward would never have killed anyone on purpose. He was an honorable, decent man."

"Did Edward ever talk about the accident?"

"He told me what happened. After going over and over it in his mind, he was sure he couldn't have prevented it. It was twilight on a rainy night. He didn't see Cyril standing in the middle of the street until the last minute. Edward stomped on the brake, but the car lurched, and he lost control, rammed into Cyril. He never meant to do it. Clare must have imagined he sped up. She's an actor. She probably doesn't know when pretending ends."

"I know Nigel was involved in the fainting game too. And, like Edward, he found it hard to forget and get on with his life."

"Nigel was Cyril's right-hand man. He did what he was told. That's why Edward didn't consider Nigel the steady hand that some of his political colleagues did. He thought, at best, Nigel was a weak man, at worst a cruel one, not fit for any important role in government. I don't know why I was taken in by Nigel's phony emails. He knew Edward's opinion of him and resented it."

"Was Edward planning to explain why he was so opposed to Nigel? Was he going to finally reveal the names of the boys who played the fainting game?"

"If he was, he never said a word about it to me. It sounds highly unlikely. Edward was not vindictive." Beryl turned into a tree-lined driveway that led to a massive stone house and parked. "Here we are," she said with obvious relief. She turned to Emily. "Oddly enough, I feel better for having talked with you. This is not a topic I can discuss with my friends, is it? And, unlikely as it seems, maybe you can help the police find Edward's killer. I want to see his death avenged. Whether it turns out to be Nigel or Clare or whoever. You have an unusual slant on the case."

"I'll try my best to help the police."

After climbing out of the car, Jack looked up at the imposing home and put his arm around Emily. "I can picture your mom living here. We could visit her often."

Beryl cast him a skeptical look. "Do you want to see the interior?"

"Love to," Emily said. Now that she had the information she had come for, she could enjoy the house tour.

Beryl led them around to the back of the house. "I want you to see the patio, then we can go inside through the French doors." Even though she clearly didn't believe they were prospective buyers, Beryl was launching into her usual spiel. "The living room has just been redecorated," she said as she led them inside. She directed their attention to the walls in soothing shades of cream and beige, a traditional fireplace with a marble surround and tall arched windows opening onto an enormous lawn.

Oohing and ahhing, Emily resolved to buy Power Ball tickets that might transform her into a rich landowner. She took photos with her phone. "I'll send these to mother. She'll love it."

"I can imagine." Beryl looked at her watch.

That afternoon, while Jack worked on his article at the desk, Emily settled in an armchair by the window and called her mother to tell her about the magnificent home for sale. "You might receive some brochures in the mail because I had to pretend you wanted to buy a home in the Cotswolds. I told the real estate agent how much you love Penelope Keith."

'I do, but, oh my heavens, I can't leave my home and traipse off to England. I have my dear grandchildren, and Zumba and Aqua Aerobics. I couldn't possibly go. You'd better set this person straight. I hope you're not trying to get rid of me. Ship me off to foreign lands."

"No, no, it was just a ruse to talk to this person. I'll explain when I get home. How is Stanley?" Emily remembered to ask about her dog, now in her mother's loving care.

"I bought him a tunnel so he could get started practicing his agility in your backyard."

"How did that go?"

"Less said the better."

"He doesn't like it?"

"He wouldn't go into the damn thing, so I tempted him with his toy duck, tossed it right in the middle. Poor Stanley was distraught, whining and peering into the tunnel. But he wouldn't crawl inside. So, I showed him how to do it and I got stuck."

Emily tried not to laugh. She was glad her mother couldn't see her face.

"Your next-door neighbor Milt had to pull me out. I've never been so embarrassed. I think agility might not be Stanley's sport."

"I believe walkies are his favorite sport."

"Enough about Stanley. I want to hear about your wedding plans. You and Jack must be working it all out together, right?"

"Don't worry. It's under control."

"It's not a crisis to be controlled. A wedding is a wonderful celebration. It won't plan itself. If you're too busy, I'd be happy to take on the job. In fact, I have a fabulous idea about where to have it. Somewhere even grander than Vanessa's castle. I could set the date, get plans rolling…"

"Oh, my God, no. Don't worry. We'll take care of it."

After she ended the call, Emily sighed with relief. "Whew, that was close. Mom wanted to take over our wedding."

Jack laughed. "You stopped her in her tracks, I assume."

That evening Emily and Jack ate dinner at the Windmill Inn, a 17th century inn with dark beamed ceilings. Sitting before the huge brick fireplace, Emily and Jack were enjoying fish and chips.

"Trying to solve this mystery has made me ravenous," Emily said, wolfing down a bite of the flakey fish so big his tail flopped over the end of the plate.

Jack agreed. "Moby Dick here is very tasty." They ate in silence for a few minutes and then, their first pangs of hunger satisfied, slowed down and began to talk as they nibbled at the rest of their meal.

"Okay, let's review," Jack said. What have you got—besides your fear that Nigel is the killer?"

"Clare has a strong motive. She's always believed Edward killed her brother. She has an alibi for the night Edward died, but maybe she administered a slow acting poison earlier. We don't know."

"Who else?"

"Beryl. She did sound convincing today, but she's still a suspect. We only have her word for it that she had a wonderful relationship with her husband. It's odd that she was so quick to believe emails from a man she knew was his enemy."

"Don't forget Sophie," Jack said. "She says she planted snakes at Clare's request, nothing more, but she did have the opportunity to kill Edward."

"On the other hand, she had no motive and has always claimed to be opposed to violent means," Emily said.

"True."

"And there's Fiona," Emily said. "She could have been at the Inn. Maybe she wanted to frame Sophie. We know she resented her for refusing to take her on as a client, but the motive seems a bit thin. You'd think she'd direct her anger toward the doctor who treated her husband rather than Sophie."

"Oh, sure. Everyone always blames the doc."

Emily patted his hand. "The person with the strongest motive would arguably be the parents of the boy who was killed, Arthur Farraday."

"I can't imagine why his parents would take revenge now after so many years."

"Nor can I. But I'd like to talk to them. They may have some helpful information."

"The headmaster told you where they live, didn't he?"

"Yes, in Avebury. It's a two-hour drive from here. It would fit in perfectly with my feature article on short trips from London."

"A bit far, isn't it?

"Not really. In my article, I could suggest a trip from London through the Cotswold villages, to Stratford on Avon, down to Avebury, then back to London. It would make an excellent two-week trip."

Chapter 18

Emily and Jack drove for two hours through rolling hills, a patchwork of green and gold, until they reached Avebury village, a town set within a Neolithic site, consisting of three stone circles enclosed by a henge, which Emily knew from her research was a wide ditch and bank.

Emily drew in her breath at the sight of huge lichen-covered rocks arranged in a vast circle spanning both sides of the road. Down the street, she saw a wooden sign swinging in the breeze, "Farraday's Crystal Emporium."

"Let's look at the stones first," Emily suggested. She was in no hurry to talk to Arthur's parents. Once their car was parked in the lot, Jack and Emily crossed the road to the entrance of the henge. Emily lifted the latch of the wooden fence and led the way into the muddy field. Huge rough stones, impressive and ancient, loomed over them. Emily placed her palm against the lichen-covered rock, hoping to feel some mysterious power, but it was just cold. "No one knows the real history of these stones," Emily said. She thought of the ancient Britons who had created this amazing site and wondered what it had meant to them. She knew that building Avebury was a tremendous achievement. It required organized labor—many people using leather straps to hoist huge Saracen stones onto wooden rollers, then to pull them into place and erect them. "Archeologists think they know *how* they did it but not why," Emily told Jack.

"Very impressive in any case."

Emily wandered among the stones, trying to picture the prehistoric people who had erected them. She knew they weren't primitive cave dwellers but farmers who looked just like modern Brits, but dressed in animal skins, woven linen and wool. They traded goods, collaborated on building the stone circles and presumably held ceremonies here.

Emily pulled out her red notebook.

Travelers' Tip: "If you plan to visit a prehistoric site in Britain, consider Avebury. Unlike Stonehenge, it has no tollbooth, no crush of tourists. You can walk among the stones, touch them, even lean against them. Its stone circles were erected about 4,000 years ago, probably for ceremonial purposes.

Emily shot photos for her article, then took Jack's arm. "Let's go to the shop and talk to the Farradays. I'm dreading it. It won't be easy to bring up the loss of their boy."

"You don't have to do this," Jack said, putting his arm around her.

"I know," Emily said. But she felt she had no choice. The Farradays might be at the heart of the mystery.

Emily and Jack crossed the street and walked down a narrow lane until they came to a brick building where crystals, amulets and books about Celts and prehistoric rituals were displayed in the window. As they opened the door, bells tinkled and kept on ringing their tunes long after Emily and Jack were inside the shop.

A thin woman with long hair streaked with gray, tied back with a ribbon laced with beads, was behind the counter. She wore a long skirt, embroidered blouse and a crystal amulet on a leather thong around her neck. A heavy-set man, balding like a monk, was in the back of the shop, placing merchandise on the shelf. He wore a tunic, baggy brown slacks, and sandals.

"Welcome," the woman said, clasping her hands in prayer position and nodding. "You've come to experience the power of the henge. Blessings."

"Thank you. I'm Emily Swift, a travel writer for an American newspaper. I'm working on an article about interesting day trips from London." She planned to work up to her real objective gradually.

"You've chosen well. Let me know if I can help you."

Emily looked over the displays of polished crystals, picking them up and admiring their beauty. Presently, the woman wandered over to her side and looked intently at her face. Finally, she smiled and said, "For you, I suggest the rose quartz." She picked up a pink translucent stone. "It brings peace and love, opens your heart so negative feelings fade away and you can let love into your heart. If anything is standing in your way, this will help. We have a rose quartz bracelet too." The woman picked up a bracelet of round pink beads and held it out. "These crystals have the power to do you good."

"It's lovely," Emily said, taking the bracelet. "I'd like to buy it." She wished rose quartz had the power to whisk away her reluctance to make wedding plans. She didn't understand why she kept delaying. Nothing was standing in her way. Emily sighed. She handed over the bracelet. "You're Mrs. Farraday, aren't you?"

"Good guess," said her husband with a smirk as he walked toward them, hitching up his trousers.

The woman glanced at him and frowned. "Yes, I'm Faith Farraday and this is my husband, Evan."

"Your wife drag you here, mate?" Evan asked Jack.

Jack shrugged. There was no good answer to that question.

"I have another reason for coming here." Emily glanced at a photo of a smiling boy on the wall between a plaque of the Green Man and an aerial photo of the henge.

Evan followed her gaze. "What reason?" He looked wary.

"Is that your son?"

"Yes," Faith murmured. "That's our Arthur."

Emily reached out, almost touching Faith's arm. "I know it must be painful to talk about him, but I'm investigating the death of Edward Westley, and I think what happened to your boy at Blanchley Hall could have a bearing on the case."

Faith drew back. "Are you police then?"

"No, but a friend has asked me to help make sure the wrong person isn't convicted."

"We keep to ourselves," Evan said. "Who put you onto us?"

"Mr. Henley told us where to find you."

Evan snorted.

"He's been kind to us," Faith said. "You know he has, Evan. Mr. Henley comes down every year and visits Arthur's grave, lays down white roses. At first, he just slipped into the churchyard on his own, didn't call on us. He wasn't sure if he'd be welcome, you see. But it wasn't his fault, was it? He was devastated, poor man." She sighed and turned to Emily. "What can we do to help you, Ms. Swift?"

"Do call me Emily. Is there a teashop nearby? I'd like to ask you a few questions if it's not too painful."

"Course it's bloody painful," Evan said. "What do you think?"

Ignoring him, Faith said, "We have a patio out back. I'll make a cup of tea. I like to talk about Arthur and remember him, the way he was. We all grieve in our own way. It's too much for Evan." She turned to her husband. "Will you watch the shop while I'm out back?"

"Won't be much to watch. Tour bus won't be here for an hour."

"So…. you will then?"

Evan shrugged. "Sure."

"If that's the case, let's go for a pint," Jack suggested to Evan "You can close up shop for a bit, can't you?"

Evan looked startled, then nodded. "Yeah. Sure. Why not?"

"We don't drink alcohol," Faith said.

"That's fine. We can have a soda then," Jack said.

Emily was pretty sure this wasn't going to happen. Evan was already putting up the closed sign.

Behind the shop was a small courtyard with a flagstone floor, enclosed by a tall hedge, where wind chimes tinkled, and birds flocked to the feeders. Faith brought out a tray with two cups of tea and an oddly shaped loaf of dark bread that looked extremely nutritious, packed as it was with dates, nuts and whole wheat flour. "It's homemade," Faith said unnecessarily.

"Mmmm, delicious," Emily lied, nibbling on a corner. Chocolate would have made all the difference.

"I'd like to hear about your son," Emily said.

The woman beamed. "Arthur was a lovely lad. His father said he was too trusting for his own good, not foxy enough. He wrote poems, loved to read and draw. He wasn't outgoing, not what you'd call an athlete or a leader. This bothered Ethan. But Arthur was devoted to his two best friends and said he didn't need anyone else. Edward was one of those dear friends. They spent holidays at each other's homes.

"You must have heard what happened to Edward," Emily said gently.

"Yes. His death was a horrible shock. We couldn't believe it when it came on the telly. I thought of going to the funeral even though we hadn't seen him in years. Ethan wouldn't hear of it. He blamed Edward for refusing to tell us what really happened to Arthur. We were like a second family to Edward, or so we thought, but he shut us out. Well, he was just a lad. I know it wasn't easy for him to keep mum. Boys have their code of silence at that age. I saw the tears in his eyes."

"Did he ever reach out to you later?"

"No. I wish he had."

"And the other boy, the third?"

"Stephen Billings. The three of them were inseparable. I thought they would be lifelong friends. Now they're all dead."

Emily was startled. "Stephen too?" She had wondered if a killer was targeting the boys who had been involved. Now that seemed more likely. "When did he die?"

"Just last year, but he'd been going downhill for a long time. Stephen stayed in touch with us through the years. He was the one who told us what happened. Cyril forced him and Arthur to play the fainting game. Edward watched, but he didn't participate. The school didn't give us details, just said that there had been an accident while a group of boys were roughhousing.

"Every time Stephen came to visit, he was in a bit worse shape. He dropped out of Oxford his first term. His parents died not long after. He started drinking too much, finally ended up homeless, using drugs. He killed himself last year. I don't know whether it was on purpose. He overdosed. The last time Stephen came to visit us, he admitted that he was the boy who first pulled the cord. He was terrified of Cyril. He pulled the cord but not hard enough to make Arthur faint. Cyril kept yelling at him. Stephen was hoping Arthur would fake it. Finally, Cyril grabbed the cord himself."

"How awful. You must have been furious at Cyril."

"He was just a boy. By the time I found out what he had done, Cyril was dead. Killed in a road accident. If he had lived, he might have changed. Bullies tend to be insecure."

"That's very charitable. Most of the people I've met in this investigation want revenge."

"Revenge just continues the cycle of violence." Faith held out her arm to show her crystal bracelet of lavender, pink and blue beads. "Amethyst and smoky quartz help to heal grief. Blue lace agate neutralizes anger." She traced her finger along the pale blue stone with its striated bands of white and shades of blue. "Arthur wouldn't want revenge to be his legacy. After his death, Evan and I had to find a way to keep going. We lived in a suburb of London at the time. I was a teacher and Ethan worked double shifts at the motor factory. We knew how smart Arthur was. The stories he wrote! He could have been a serious author, maybe won the Booker Prize. So, we'd been working long hours to keep Arthur at Blanchley Hall. Even with his scholarship we had to make sacrifices. Ironic, isn't it? If he'd gone to the comprehensive, he'd be alive. We didn't know he was being bullied. He never said."

Faith took a sip of tea and drew a breath, pulling herself together. "After Arthur died, we didn't see the point of trying to make a lot of money. We moved to Avebury and used an inheritance from my aunt, who had just died, to buy this little shop. I had always been Church of England. Didn't go often. When Arthur died, I found no comfort because the vicar kept talking about how we'd meet Arthur again in heaven. I don't believe that. Wish I did. Arthur lives in my heart and my memory. That has to be enough.

"For some reason Avebury seemed healing to me. Many of the people who come here are seekers, people who have lost confidence in mainstream religion, but are looking for meaning or comfort. Modern-day Druids hold ceremonies here."

"Are you a Druid then?"

"No, but I'm drawn to ancient paths of healing. Crystals and such. I find peace walking among the stones, connecting with the earth. What about you, Emily? Do you go to church?"

Taken aback by the personal question, Emily paused, but she had to answer. The woman's pale blue eyes were fixed on her.

"I do … sometimes. I like to be in a community of people who share my beliefs and values, singing and praying together, reacting to things going on in the world, trying to find meaning and ways to help others. I believe in the power of myths and rites and traditions. As to hoping for a reunion with my Granny in heaven, I doubt it. But I'm not ruling anything out."

"Seekers are part of an old, old tradition," Faith said. "Avebury must have been tremendously important to the prehistoric people who built it with such great effort. It was used for rituals and ceremonies, probably to do with fertility, birth and death. These people must have been trying to make sense of their world, a precursor of medieval people who labored for years to build Cathedrals in Europe."

"I admire you for finding a healthy way to heal and a place that seems right for you."

"Avebury has helped me. But most important to me and to Ethan is the Good Friends' Project. Ethan and I founded the anti-bullying society years ago. I prepared a syllabus for the schools. Ethan is the one who goes into the classrooms to present it. Boys respond to him better than to me. We set up web pages to support teenagers and parents. So much bullying these days is on social media. I want the anti-bullying campaign to be Arthur's legacy. Maybe he would have written books that opened people's hearts and made them more compassionate. I can't do that. I don't have his talent. I do what I can."

The doorbells began their cacophony as Jack and Ethan came into the shop. "We're back, love!" Ethan called.

"Thank you, Faith," Emily said, reaching out to her.

On the drive back to Stratford, Emily told Jack about her conversation with Faith. "She found a way to help herself and her husband survive a terrible loss. I can't imagine her harming Edward or anyone else. What about her husband?"

"Ethan's not into the crystals and ancient myths, but he loves his wife and he's following her game plan. He still blames himself and his boy for what happened."

With commendable accuracy, Jack recounted the story that Ethan had told him over a pint of ale at the Red Lion.

Ethan's Story

"If I had taught him to box or wrestle or some damn thing, maybe he could have stood up to that little thug, that goddam Cyril," Ethan said. "Faith wanted me to let Arthur find his own way. She said he was fine, just different from me. But he wasn't fine. He couldn't say 'no' when he had to."

"It's tough for kids to do that," Jack said.

"I understand that now. But crazy as it sounds, right after Arthur died, I used to get angry at him. I wanted to yell: 'Didn't you think of your mum? Couldn't you have stood up to that little sod for her sake?' Then I felt guilty. Raging at my poor boy.

"Faith's right. The only thing we can do now is try to help other lads who are pushed by bullies to play stupid games, take drugs… whatever. I wouldn't have thought of it on my own. Faith did the research, came up with the anti-bullying plan, contacted the schools.

"Schools need help. I think Blanchley Hall was lax. That damn Henley may be sorry now, but he was looking the other way when those boys were playing a deadly game. Sipping his port, was he? Nodding off over poetry in the library? No matter what he says, it happened on his watch.

"The schools were doing naught. So, I agreed with Faith. We had to do something. Using her lesson plan, I go into the schools. When I see a boy snicker while I'm talking, I walk up to him, stand by his desk, look down at him with all the contempt I feel. 'Funny, is it?' I ask him. 'A boy dead and you laughing.' The boy always smirks, but finally he looks down at his hands and his face turns red. I can see his mates straighten up, see that he isn't quite as tough as they thought."

"Good for you, Ethan," Jack said. "We have the same problem in the states. I'm working on an article now on the long-lasting effects of childhood violence and trauma. Illnesses in adults can have their roots in childhood experiences. So, what you're doing is tremendously important. I try to watch for signs that my young patients are being bullied and work with their parents to help them. The problem is kids don't want anyone to know."

"I understand that now. At first, I didn't see why Arthur didn't tell me what was going on. You wouldn't think I'd have to forgive my boy, but I did. The henge and the chunks of crystal that Faith puts so much store in did naught for me, but as I read her lesson plan and went into the schools, I began to understand what should have been bloody obvious. Kids that age want to belong. They need to be taught how to stand up to a bully."

Jack finished his account of his pint at the pub with Ethan. "I felt sorry for the poor guy and impressed by the way he was handling it."

"Poor soul," Emily said.

"Ethan still has anger simmering below the surface, but I do think he wants to channel it in a positive direction. I don't think he's a suspect. I asked him flat out if he had any idea who would want to kill Edward. He said, 'No. We haven't seen him in years. Lots of time for him to make enemies.'"

"So, we've reached a dead end." Emily sighed. "Maybe Edward's murder isn't related to the fainting game at all."

That evening, back in their room at Adelphi House, Jack said, "I bought you a present. Hold out your hand." He dropped a small canvas bag into Emily's palm. Emily untied the pouch and emptied the smooth stones into her hand: deep orange, silver, black, and caramel streaked with brown. She read aloud the words printed on the bag: "Protection crystals: Carnelian, Labradorite, Obsidian and Tiger's Eye."

"Thank you, Jack. I hope I won't need protection, but the stones are beautiful." She hugged him. "I didn't see anything just right for you, but I bought something in the shop too. I thought I should after Faith was so kind. "Look at this bracelet." Emily held up her wrist to show the rose quartz beads. "Faith told me they open your heart to love. Luckily, I'm already rich in love." Emily smiled at Jack. She didn't mention Faith's claim that quartz would sweep away anything standing in her way. Emily had no doubt that she dearly loved Jack and always would. She wasn't sure why she kept putting off setting a date for their wedding.

Chapter 19

Emily woke up with a memory replaying itself in her mind so vividly it seemed real. She was sitting in the kitchen of the house where she had lived when she was ten years old, listening to a litany of her mother's complaints about her father. Finally, she asked her mom why in the world she had married him if he was as bad as all that.

She heard her mother's answer. "Your Father and I got along beautifully when we were dating. And for years we had tremendous fun together, especially when we went out for dinner or when we went on vacation. Remember all the good times we had in that cabin on the North Shore? The responsibility of the house and bills to pay and our different approach to life caused most of our fights. His dangerous job as a police officer didn't help either. Every time he walked out the door, I worried that he'd be killed. The fear ate away at me. We started to quarrel all the time. Finally, your father just walked out."

Emily came fully awake. It took her a moment to realize where she was and drag herself back to the present. Her memory had been so vivid, her mother's voice so clear. She turned to look at Jack, sound asleep, lying on his back, his arms folded across his chest. *No worries*, Emily thought with relief. She and Jack already lived together. They parented a large rescue dog, Stanley. They had no screaming, yelling fights over money or how to take care of the house or train the dog. Jack was a physician not a cop who was in danger every day. Emily smiled. Sometimes a memory you can't even recall paralyzes you. Then you pull it up and say, "Pffft, what was that all about? No problem." Maybe the rose crystal really did sweep away fears that were hidden deep in her oldest memories. In any case, Emily realized that fear of repeating her parents' experience had lost its power once her memory rose into the light of day. Now that she knew what had been holding her back, she could look forward to her wedding.

Over a lovely breakfast of coffee, scrambled eggs with chives, a toasted crumpet, hot cross bun, sausage, bacon and a bowl of fresh fruit, Emily told Jack about her dream. "I had no idea why I've been so reluctant to start planning our wedding. I just didn't want anything to spoil our relationship and cause us to end up like my bickering parents."

Jack reached across the table and took her hand, stroking her engagement ring with his thumb. "And now you're not worried?"

"No. We're not like my parents. Not at all. We're going to be great."

Jack grinned. "Yes, we are."

"I'll call Father Cronin and set the date," Emily said. "Nothing stands in our way now." Emily snapped her bracelet. "Who knows, maybe the quartz helped."

As they stood up to leave Jack put his arms around Emily, pulled her close, and once they were in the quiet hallway, kissed her.

As they walked to the car, Jack chuckled. "Your mom will be over the moon."

"Oddly enough, last time I called her, Mom said we have an amazing opportunity for a wedding venue even grander than Vanessa's 'castle,' as she calls it."

Jack laughed. "Tell her to relax. Our church will be grand enough for us."

Emily knew their time in England was drawing to a close. It was time to finish up her research. So, she and Jack headed to Anne Hathaway's Cottage, a charming thatch roofed farmhouse, timber framed in the Tudor style.

Jack whistled as they pulled into the parking lot. "Not exactly a cottage. It's huge."

"Yes, it has twelve rooms, lots of chimneys and beautiful gardens," Emily said. "Anne Hathaway, the woman Shakespeare married, grew up here. Her family must have been prosperous."

Inside the cozy house with its latticed windows and period furniture, Emily saw the courting chair where Will wooed Anne when she was twenty-six and he eighteen. Not for the first time, Emily wished she knew their story. Anne was pregnant at the time. Was it a shotgun wedding? Did Will feel obliged to marry her? Or did he love her despite the age difference? "Age cannot wither her nor custom stale her infinite variety," he wrote. Maybe like Cleopatra, Anne had charms that transcended the age difference and continued to captivate him all his life. Emily hoped so.

After touring the house, Emily took photos as she and Jack explored the gardens. The knot garden of lavender was just starting to bud, tulips and daffodils were already in bloom. They followed the woodland walk, reveling in the blue sky, listening to birdsong. Emily tried to immerse herself in the Tudor world, to think of Will and Anne walking hand in hand on this very path, but disappointment at failing to solve the crime bedeviled her.

She and Jack drove on to the nearby farm in Wilmcote where Mary Arden, Shakespeare's mother, lived as a girl. Emily jotted in her little red notebook.

> ***Travelers' Tip:*** *Be sure to visit Anne Hathaway's cottage with its beautiful gardens, then go on to Mary Arden's farm where Shakespeare's mother lived. This is a working farm where costumed guides milk cows, cut wood, feed chickens. Even if you're not a Shakespeare fan, you'll enjoy stepping back into fifteenth century England.*

In her traveler's tip, Emily didn't mention the falconry demonstration, which had fallen flat. The owl soared off from the falconer's glove and sought refuge in the barn, where it settled high in the rafters, ignoring the falconer's pleas and bribes of raw meat.

"Nigel's man has better luck," Jack said as they headed to the parking lot. "Where to?"

"Let's go back to our room. I have to finish my articles." Emily sighed. "Our trip's almost over."

"And you hate to leave the case unsolved and spoil your perfect record."

"True."

"But you did what Vanessa wanted. You found out the identity of the woman who impersonated Beryl. That should be enough to clear Sophie from suspicion."

"I guess I'll have to be content with a modest success." Emily realized that delving deeper into the mystery might uncover a truth that she didn't want to face.

When they returned to Adelphi House, Emily called Vanessa and told her about her visit to Avebury.

"Too bad the Farradays turned out to be so nice," Vanessa said. "I was hoping they'd be prime suspects and get poor Nigel off the hook."

"I don't think Nigel's on the hook," Emily lied. She couldn't think of a more likely suspect at the moment.

"Sophie's here with me. Can I put you on speakerphone?"

"Yes, of course." Emily and Sophie exchanged quick greetings.

"How's Jack doing?" Vanessa asked. "I hope he doesn't mind playing Watson."

"Not at all. He's eager to help solve the case, although Jack doesn't like to be cast in the supporting role of Watson. And he's busy with his own projects. He's almost finished with an article for the state medical journal, and he's very concerned about his Irish cousin Nora. Apparently, she's getting way too thin. Brendan confided in him when they were at the races. They've been emailing back and forth ever since. He wants to help in some way but can't imagine what he could do."

"He's a terrific guy, Emily. I'm so glad you found him."

"Me too. You'll be my bridesmaid, won't you, Vanessa?"

"Of course."

"So, what were you telling Vanessa before I came on the call?" Sophie interrupted. Have you made any progress in the investigation?"

"Oh, Sophie, not much. I was just telling Vanessa that Jack and I went to see the parents of the boy who died during the fainting game. If they believed Edward had a hand in their son's death, they could have had a motive, but they don't. They're very kind, new-agey folks who live in Avebury and go around to schools teaching children about the evils of bullying and how to resist it."

"Not suspects then?" Sophie asked.

"No. But I did find out there was a third boy who was involved in the Farraday boy's death. Stephen Billings. Apparently, he was a close friend of Edward and Arthur and, like them, he was bullied by Cyril and his followers." Emily didn't mention that Nigel was one of those followers.

"Could Stephen's family be involved?" Vanessa asked.

"I don't think so. His parents died before Stephen did. He died of a drug overdose just last year. No one knows if it was deliberate or an accident. Or if it was related to the fainting game at all."

"Good work, Emily," Sophie said. "You've done your best. Now you can go back to Minneapolis with no regrets. I'll be fine. The police let me go after they questioned Clare and she admitted she impersonated Beryl and hired me to plant the snakes. Since the snakes weren't the cause of his death anyway, Clare might not be in much trouble either. We'll probably never know who poisoned Edward."

"I'll look into it a little more," Emily said. "I still worry that someone could be targeting all those who were involved in the fainting game. Maybe Stephen had a friend who knows something."

"The police will sort it out. You've done what Vanessa asked. Cleared my name. I am grateful to you, Emily," Sophie said. "We'll stay in touch. I have your email address. And I'll friend you on Facebook."

"Of course," Emily said, but she couldn't let go of the investigation, not yet.

Later that afternoon, Jack came into their room, where Emily was working on her article. "How was your hike?" Emily asked him.

"Excellent. I tramped for three miles and was still forging ahead. I only came back because I got a mysterious text from my cousin Brendan. He says he needs my help on a very hush-hush matter. 'Thank God we have a doc in the family,' he says. I wonder what that means."

"Uh oh. What do you think he wants? Ireland is full of doctors. I hope it isn't something shady. I wouldn't like to have to visit you in an Irish prison."

"It probably concerns Nora. As you know, Brendan's afraid she's becoming anorexic, but I don't know how I could help." Emily noticed the worry line between his brows.

"Brendan's email says it will just take a day or two at the most. He'll have a ticket on Ryanair waiting for me at Gatwick. I don't know why Brendan would buy me a ticket. It's not as though I can't afford my own ticket."

"Maybe he wants you to realize just how much he wants you there. It must be serious."

"You're probably right. 'Just come as quick as you can,' he says. 'Don't mention it to Uncle Valentine.'"

"Maybe Brendan wants to stage an intervention and try to get Nora into treatment," Emily said.

"That makes sense. Uncle Valentine wouldn't be helpful since he denies there's a problem. And Brendan did say Nora looks up to me. I'm going to call him."

The phone call didn't go through. No connection. Jack tried several times without success.

"Even if his message is a bit mysterious, I can't say no, Emily. The Irish Flynns were so good to me the summer I spent with them when I was in college. They're a great, fun-loving bunch and very welcoming. Do you mind? Ryanair can get me there and back in a day or two. I'll be back in time for us to fly home together on Wednesday."

"Of course, you should go. Especially if you can help Brendan and Nora. As a doc, you might have credibility that her family lacks. Go for it."

"We could drive up to London together later this afternoon."

"I'd like to see Vanessa again and say goodbye before I go. I'll finish up my article here while you're gone." Emily quickly checked her phone for travel information. "Why don't you take the train to Gatwick Airport? It takes less than an hour. When you get there, you might be able to connect with Brendan and find out more about what's going on, figure out how long you'll need to be in Ireland."

"I'll call you as soon as I know."

"After I hear that you're on your way back from Dublin, I'll drive up to London. We can meet back at the Grande Royale Hotel and stay there a night before we fly home."

"That would work. Will you be okay driving all that way in traffic on the wrong side of the road?"

"Sure. After three weeks, it's begun to seem normal to me. Well, almost normal."

Jack hugged her. "I have to confess I'm glad our investigation has stalled. I won't have to worry about you."

"No, you can worry about your distant cousins for a change."

After Emily saw Jack off on the train to Gatwick, she went back to their room, finished her last article and emailed it to George, her editor. Feeling that she had been sufficiently dutiful, she then looked up information on Stephen Billings on her computer. She found an old news item about his parents' death dated a year after the fatal incident at Blanchley Hall.

Bibury Chronicle
  Agatha and Earl Billings of Bibury,
  both 46 years old, were killed in a
  single-car collision Thursday. They died

instantly after their automobile hit an embankment. They leave behind a son Stephen and a daughter Sophia.

There was a photo of the Billings family, the doomed boy Stephen standing between his parents. A girl about ten years old stood in front of them. Emily zoomed in on the only survivor of the Billings family. Sophie? It couldn't be? Could it? The name was not uncommon. But even in this grainy photo, the child's face looked familiar.

Emily's heart was pounding. She called Vanessa. "I've got a quick question for you. We're not on speakerphone, are we?"

"No. Why do you ask?"

"Is Sophie with you?"

"No, she left a while ago."

"Was she ever married? Could she be using an ex-husband's last name?"

"If she ever married, she never mentioned it. Why do you ask?"

"No reason. I just wonder if she ever used another last name."

"Not since I've known her."

"Okay. Thanks."

Emily let out her breath. Good. So, it was probably just a coincidence. Emily started to pack. But the image of the face of the ten-year-old child hovered in the back of her mind. It looked a lot like Sophie. Especially the expression in her eyes and the pointed little chin.

Knowing it was a longshot, Emily typed "Sophia Morton" in her search engine. Listed first on the screen were a string of articles about Sophie's temp agency, then as she scrolled down Emily saw an obituary from the *Chipping Campden Herald* dated a little more than a year ago.

Sophia Morton, age 55, longtime resident of Chipping Campden, died Wednesday after suffering a fatal heart attack. She is survived by her niece and namesake Sophia, whom she adopted after the child's parents died in an automobile accident. Mrs. Morton was preceded in death by her husband Earl, her sister, Agatha Billings, and nephew, Stephen Billings.

The obituary went on to list the dead woman's many activities in her community and a notice of a funeral service.

Emily was stunned. This changed everything. Sophie's brother was Stephen Billings, the poor boy who never overcame his guilt and sorrow at the death of his best friend during the fainting game. He had left Oxford and was living on his own when his parents died. Then he slid into a depression that ended in his death.

Emily shivered. Sophie had the means, the opportunity and the motive. She must have killed Edward. Her computer skills would have allowed her to make it seem that emails to Beryl came from Nigel. She meant to frame him because he was Cyril's friend.

Emily wished Jack were here so she could tell him. She tried to call but he didn't answer. She left a message on his phone. "Jack, I know who did it. Call me."

Emily knew she had to go to the police. She definitely would not confront someone as dangerous as Sophie on her own. But the news would be crushing to Vanessa. Emily had to tell her what she'd discovered before she went to the police. Once the police knew Sophie had a strong motive, they would investigate her thoroughly and find the evidence they needed to convict. Chillingworth Manor was on the way to the police station so Emily could stop to see Vanessa, then go on to London, her work well done.

Emily tried to reach Vanessa but her call went straight to voice mail, so she left a message. "Vanessa, I know for sure that Nigel's innocent. So sorry I didn't take your word for it. Anyway, can I come over tonight? I'll stop to say goodbye on my way to London. Call me."

Presently, she heard a ping and opened up a text message from Vanessa; "Can't talk now. Yes, do come. I'll be in the garden. We'll have a glass of wine."

Chapter 20

That evening, Emily was surprised to find the windows dark at Chillingworth Manor. It must be the staff's night off. She followed the path along the side of the manor to the garden where Vanessa said she'd meet her. Behind the house, floodlights shone on the rose garden and maze, making them as bright as at midday.

"Vanessa!" Emily called, but there was no answer.

Then she heard Nigel. "Come on into the maze."

"Nigel, where are you?" Emily took a step into the boxwood maze. Vanessa must be waiting for her in the gazebo.

"Come on. You can find your way," Nigel encouraged her.

"What's going on, Nigel? Where's Vanessa?" She followed the first turn of the maze, going in the direction of his voice. Could she really find her way alone? Maybe Nigel was leading her there. She just had to catch up with him. Vanessa would be pouring the wine, lighting the candles.

"Keep going," Nigel called. "You're doing fine."

Emily followed another turn, then came to a fork in the greenery and chose one of two paths at random. It led to a dead end where a topiary shaped like a small rabbit stood in a niche. Nigel must be playing some sort of joke, but she was not amused. Emily turned back and went down the other path.

"There's no escape." Nigel sounded threatening now. "You won't get away." Emily heard footsteps, a whoosh of wind. She wanted to get out of the maze, but it was too late, greenery closed around her. The path was narrower now and branches scratched her arms. She heard savage howling, footsteps coming closer. It must be Digger and she had no biscuits in her pocket.

Emily realized she must have been wrong about Sophie. Nigel was the killer after all. And now he was after her.

"Oops not that way. You're lost. Well and truly lost." Nigel gave an insane cackle.

Vanessa had told Emily the only way through the maze was to look for red threads that signaled the correct turns. Emily took a calming breath. She saw a red loop tied to a branch and turned. She broke into a run now that she knew the direction she had to follow. She'd head straight to the secret doorway as soon as she reached the gazebo.

"There's danger in the maze." A crazed laugh rang out. "Danger!" The dog's howling grew louder. Digger must be almost upon her.

Emily turned again in the direction indicated by the red thread. Suddenly the floodlights shut off and Emily was plunged into darkness. She placed her hand on the hedge and slowly crept along feeling for the threads but not finding any. She made her way through two more turns, then, at last, stepped into the center of the maze. As a cloud drifted away from the moon, its ghostly white light shone on Sophie, standing in front of the gazebo, dressed all in black.

"Thank God, you're here," Emily gasped.

Then she saw that Sophie was holding a medieval battle axe. Emily recognized the lethal weapon that had been displayed in the great hall, the axe with a tip as sharp as a sword's blade.

She heard Nigel's voice say, "Come into the maze." His coaxing tone was the same as it had been at the beginning, encouraging rather than crazy and terrifying.

"It's a recording," Emily said as the truth hit her. No one was chasing her. She had run straight into danger. "It must be on a loop and it's beginning again."

"Very astute of you. Nigel's ghost experience. He's quite proud of it. My timing was perfect, don't you think?"

"Sophie, why? Is this a joke? You can't be the killer. I don't believe it," Emily lied.

"I wish you didn't believe it. I really like you, Emily. But if you haven't figured out what happened yet, you soon will."

"If you did kill Edward, you got away with it. The police don't suspect you anymore. Even if I told them you were guilty, they wouldn't believe me. Don't press your luck. If you kill me, you're sure to pay for both murders."

"Everyone will think Nigel killed both of you. The medieval touch." Sophie raised the battle axe.

"Why? You didn't even know Edward Westley."

"Don't play dumb, Emily. You know he was one of the boys involved in the fainting game."

"Edward knew about the game, but he wasn't an instigator. That's what I heard."

"He was my brother's best friend and he stood by and watched Cyril force my brother to play that wretched game and make him pull the cord around Arthur's neck. Everyone who stood by or joined in the fatal game has to suffer the consequences. Of course, they'll be severe. Two boys are dead."

"I know about Arthur Farraday. Who was the second boy?" Emily knew but she wanted to keep Sophie talking.

"My brother, Stephen. He was sent down from University. He was damaged. He started drinking and fell into a depression. He died when he was just thirty-one. Someone has to pay."

"Cyril has already paid. Edward killed him. Whether it was on purpose or by accident nobody knows. Clare thinks it was deliberate. Murder in fact."

"How ironic. If I had known that Edward had killed Cyril, I would have spared his life. I would have done what Clare wanted—frighten him with the snakes and left it at that."

"You didn't know?"

"Of course not. I was only ten years old. I didn't read accident reports. I'm not sure if his name would have been in the news anyway. He was only sixteen.

"When Clare came to my office, I recognized her right away even in her flimsy disguise. I'd been following her acting career, such as it was. Clare didn't have any idea who I was. The last time she'd seen me, I was a little girl and my name was different. When my aunt adopted me, I took her last name. Clare, impersonating Beryl, told me the tall tale about wanting to pay Edward back for his practical jokes. I pretended to believe her. At first, I just meant to go along with Clare's plan and frighten Edward. Then I began to be plagued by dreams. One morning I woke up with the ghost's line from Hamlet ringing in my ears. "Revenge his foul and most unnatural murder." I had played Ophelia at school, so I knew the play well. That day I began to think that I had been too much like Hamlet, hesitating to act. Clare's idea sparked one of my own. I wouldn't use poisonous snakes. There was too much risk of them being traced back to me even though I would try to prevent that. But I made sure Edward would die terrified. I put a fast-acting poison in the hip flask of brandy he always carried. I knew he'd try to steady his nerves with a quick drink. Then as paralysis crept over him, the snakes would slither on to his bed."

Emily was horrified. Sophie stood between her and the secret doorway behind the gazebo. She had to wait until Sophie moved and then she could make a dash to escape. Nigel's recorded voice was still blaring in the background. "There's danger in the maze." Suddenly, the lights flashed on again, revealing Sophie's determined face, and startling her into action. "How did that happen? I turned the lights off. Oh well, I'd better get on with it." Sophie stepped forward, brandishing the battle axe.

"I thought you didn't believe in physical violence," Emily said, backing away.

"Normally, I don't. But I make exceptions."

The baying of the hound grew so loud there seemed to be two dogs. Sophie raised the axe over her head. Emily dodged past her and started to run around the gazebo to the secret exit. Sophie was right behind her.

Suddenly, Digger bounded into the center of the maze, closely followed by Nigel. "Get her!" Nigel yelled. The dog leaped onto Sophie's back and brought her to ground. She tried to lift the battle axe and strike him, but it was too heavy; she was pinned.

Nigel grabbed his axe, twisting it out of Sophie's hand. Digger sank his teeth into Sophie's arm. She screamed, "Stop him! Call him off!"

"Easy, Digger." Nigel said. "Hold." The dog stopped biting but kept her pinned with his huge paws. "Good dog. Good boy." He tossed a couple of biscuits into the dog's open slavering mouth.

"Emily, what's going on?" Vanessa stumbled into the center of the maze, breathless, panting, her eyes wide with alarm. "Why is Nigel's recording blasting away?" She looked down at Sophie and Digger. "What's happening?"

"Sophie tried to kill me," Emily said, pointing toward the axe in Nigel's hand. "Thank God you arrived when you did. Nigel and Digger saved me from a particularly horrible death." Emily turned to Nigel,

"Thank you, thank you, Nigel. I've never been so glad to see anyone."

"We came back early," Vanessa said. "The concert wasn't really very good, so we left at the interval." She sounded stunned.

"When we got home, we heard my 'Ghost Experience' recording, saw the floodlights were on and wondered what the hell was going on," Nigel said. "I'll notify the authorities." He took out his phone and punched in the number of the police station, then turned aside to call for assistance.

Vanessa looked down at Sophie, who had given up and was lying still under Digger's great paws. "You tried to kill Emily? Why?"

"My arm's bleeding. Get that damn hellhound off me."

"Sophie was afraid I'd figured out who Edward's killer was, and she was right," Emily said. "I found out that Sophie's brother was a friend of the boy who died during the fainting game. Her brother was destroyed by guilt and killed himself. The minute I knew Sophie had a motive, I realized that she poisoned Edward and was trying to frame Nigel. She wanted your husband blamed for Edward's murder and for mine."

"That can't be true, Sophie. How could you do that to Nigel and Emily? I thought you were my friend."

"I didn't want to harm you…. or Emily either for that matter," Sophie said. "But Nigel was one of the boys who ganged up on my brother Stephen and made him play the fainting game. They forced him to join in killing his best friend. Your husband deserves to be punished."

Vanessa looked at Nigel. "Is that true?"

"I was a just a boy. I was afraid of Cyril. If I had stood up to him, I'd be the next victim. I just kept a low profile. I didn't force anyone to play the game."

"You knew what was going on and you did nothing," Sophie said. "You coward. I wanted you to be convicted of Edward's murder."

"So that's why Edward had it in for you," Vanessa said.

"That's pretty ironic since Edward stood by and watched the game himself," Nigel said. "Later he refused to tell the authorities who was involved. He wanted to rewrite history with himself as a hero, but we were all afraid of Cyril. We were just boys. We didn't dare stand up to him. None of us did. I'm not proud of it, but there it is." He ran a hand through his hair and looked away from his wife.

"Poor lamb," Vanessa said, taking his hand. "You were a victim too." Nigel sighed with relief. "And tonight, you were a hero."

"Are you going to let me bleed to death?" Sophie asked.

"No, of course not," Nigel said. "I called the police. They'll deal with you."

Emily heard a familiar yell. "Emily, where are you?" Jack's voice sounded frantic.

"Jack! Follow the red threads at each turn. I'm fine."

Presently, Jack arrived in the center of the maze and pulled Emily into his arms. "Thank God, you're safe. I realized I'd been tricked the minute I got to the airport. There was no ticket waiting for me. As you know, I haven't been able to reach anyone in Ireland. I thought something was wrong with my phone. At the airport, my call finally went through and Brendan answered. He had no idea what I was talking about. He said there was no crisis, just ongoing concern, nothing new. He hadn't emailed me. Then I knew you must be in danger so I drove back as quickly as I could. You said you were going to see Vanessa, so I came straight here."

"I need a doctor," Sophie said. "This hellhound practically bit my arm off. Get to work, Jack. I could bleed to death."

Digger growled and shifted his hairy paws.

Jack looked down at Sophie. "Hmm. Doesn't look too bad. I'll bind it up for you."

Nigel called off Digger and gave him a bone as his reward for a job well done. Jack ripped off the bottom of Sophie's shirt and wrapped the rag tightly around her bleeding arm. In the distance, sirens were wailing.

"I believe there's some wine in the gazebo," Vanessa said. "We all need something to restore our strength." Vanessa put her arm around Emily. "You're a good friend, Emily. I'm sorry I got you involved in this mess."

"Thank goodness the concert was a dud," Jack said. "Otherwise you and Nigel would have been too late to save her. I would have arrived just in time to find Emily beheaded like an unlucky queen." He could joke now that the danger was past.

The sirens' wail was becoming louder and louder.

Vanessa handed out glasses of chilled white wine to everyone but Sophie. Giddy with relief, they sipped cold wine and pieced together the events that had led them here.

"Apparently, Sophie hacked into my email to lure me out of town with the fake message from Brendan," Jack said. "How would she know to do that?" He spoke as if Sophie were not lying right there with Digger on top of her, gnawing a bone.

"She was on speaker phone when I was talking to Vanessa about your worries about Nora and Brendan," Emily said. "She knew just how to get to you."

"Sophie must have hacked into your email too, Vanessa, and sent me a message asking me to meet you in the garden," Emily said.

"How could you? I was trying to help clear your name," Vanessa said to Sophie. "I thought you were innocent."

Sophie shrugged. "Where's *my* glass of wine," I'm in a lot of pain."

"You don't deserve a drop of wine," Vanessa snapped.

The siren rose to a shriek then stopped. "Police!" a voice yelled. "Who called police? Identify yourself."

"In the maze, officers!" Nigel called out. "Follow the red threads."

Emily heard swearing and snapping branches. At last, Sgt. Norville led two other uniformed officers into the center of the maze. "Who called in an emergency?"

Jack and Nigel both spoke up.

"I called from the airport," Jack said. "I said my wife was in great danger at Chillingworth Manor."

"I called a few minutes ago to say we had subdued a confessed murderer," Nigel added.

"This woman tried to kill me," Emily said, pointing at Sophie. "She admitted she killed Edward Westley. She tried to kill me because she was afraid I'd figured out what she had done."

"That's why it is highly inadvisable for ordinary citizens to involve themselves in police matters," Norville said, glowering at her. "It's dangerous and makes our job more difficult."

Emily thought it churlish of Norville not to be the least bit grateful for her assistance in nabbing a killer.

Vanessa offered wine to Norville and his colleagues.

"This is not a garden party," Sgt. Norville snapped.

Nigel handed the battle axe to an officer who put it in an evidence bag. "This is what Sophie meant to use to whack poor Emily," he said. "She tried to make sure that Vanessa and I would be away from home. She gave us tickets to a concert of Faure's Requiem at the village church. What she didn't know was that I actually hate that sort of funereal music and could only put up with it until the interval."

"Thank God!" Emily said. "Sophie must have thought her timing was perfect. Nigel and Vanessa would arrive home tonight. The lights would be off. They would have no reason to go into the garden. When they finally found my body, Nigel would be the logical suspect because I'd have been killed with his battle axe." Emily shivered and Jack put his arm around her.

The officers helped Sophie to her feet.

"Don't cuff me. I've been badly injured. That vicious dog should be put down."

Digger glanced up at her, then returned to gnawing his bone.

"Sophie thought she had got rid of me too," Jack said. "She hacked into my email and sent me a message that seemed to come from my cousin, begging me to go to Dublin. The email said there'd be a plane ticket waiting for me at the airport. That was her mistake. When the ticket wasn't there, I realized it must be a trick. Instead of flying to Ireland, I called the police and rushed here.

"You'll all be expected to testify against the defendant," Sgt. Norville said. He turned to Sophie. "I am arresting you for the murder of Edward Westley and the attempted murder of Emily Swift." He gave the standard British notice of rights to the accused, similar to a Miranda warning.

With an officer on each side, Sophie walked back into the maze. Sgt. Norville followed.

Jack put his arm around Emily. "When I read your message saying you knew who the killer was, I was horrified," he said. "I knew you'd rush into danger."

"No, I meant to *avoid* danger, but I had to talk to Vanessa before I went to the police. When I heard your voice, Nigel, I believed you were leading me to her. Then when you started to sound threatening, I thought I had been wrong, and you must be the killer after all. Forgive me for misjudging you."

"No wonder," Nigel murmured. "That woman's devilishly clever."

"Emily, my dear friend, you were almost killed trying to help me," Vanessa said.

"Too true," Jack said. "But don't feel too bad. Emily loves the thrill of the chase, don't you, my darling?" He pulled her close and kissed the top of her head.

"As long as it ends well," Emily said. "And this time it did. We're all safe. The guilty will be punished, the innocent are cleared of suspicion, and the good dog has his bone."

THE END

ABOUT THE AUTHOR

 Like her fictional heroine, Lorrie loves to travel and learn about the history, art and culture of other lands. She grew up in Wilmette, a suburb of Chicago, graduated from Wells College in Aurora, New York, and received her MA in communication and theater arts from the University of Minnesota. For many years, she was the director of communications of the Minnesota Medical Association.

Lorrie lives in Minneapolis with her husband, close to her daughter and son and their families. In addition to travel, she enjoys Latin dance, Zumba, aqua aerobics, gardening, knitting, book group discussions and playing board games with her grandson,

A Killing in the Cotswolds: An Emily Swift Travel Mystery is the third novel in the series. Read Emily's first sleuthing adventure, *Murder on Madeline Island* and her second, *Homicide in Hawaii.* Learn more at www.lorrieholmgren.com and at www.facebook.com/lorrieholmgrenauthor

.

Made in the USA
Monee, IL
04 July 2023

38636854R00142